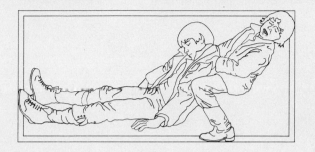

UNDER THE SAME STARS

DEAN HUGHES

Deseret Book Company
Salt Lake City, Utah
1979

For Kathleen

Preface

Under the Same Stars is a historical novel. The Williams family is my invention, as are Ollie Markley and his father and some of the minor characters among the old settlers of Jackson County, Missouri. Most of the characters, however, are based on actual people. Joseph Smith, Parley P. Pratt, Edward Partridge, Newel Knight, William W. Phelps, and Oliver Cowdery were all well-known leaders of the early Mormon Church. Lilburn Boggs, Samuel Owens, and George Lucas were actual settlers in Independence. While it was necessary for me to conjecture about what these people might have done or said in particular situations, this conjecture was based on extensive research.

The major incidents of the novel are also based on actual events. The dates, the places and events, the atmosphere of the time, are all as accurate as I could possibly make them. I based my knowledge on numerous histories and biographies, but also on unpublished diaries, journals, maps, and other resources. The individual experiences of Joseph Williams and his family, within the larger historical framework, are my creation, of course, but they represent common experiences of Mormon settlers in early Jackson County.

I have also attempted to view the explosive events in the novel with objectivity, to represent as carefully as possible the points of view of both the old settlers of Independence and the Mormons. Sometimes diary accounts differ, and in those cases it was necessary to choose that version which seemed most plausible.

I wish to acknowledge the cooperation and help of the following: Jim Kimball and the staff of the Historical Department of The Church of Jesus Christ of Latter-day Saints; the staff of the Library-Archives of the Reorganized Church of Jesus Christ of Latter Day Saints; the staff of the Library of the Missouri Historical Society; Davis Bitton, who allowed me to use his *Guide to Mormon Diaries and Autobiographies* before it was published; Max Parkin, expert on Missouri Mormon history; Phil Sadler, who advised me on the manuscript; Beatrice Ricks, who would not let me *not* write; my wife, Kathleen, and my children, Tom, Amy, and Robert, who listened to every draft of every chapter and responded honestly.

Chapter 1

The *Chieftain* suddenly lurched and it finally happened—just what Joseph and his older brother, Matthew, had been waiting for. One of the stringy filaments of tar that stretched beneath the hurricane deck of the riverboat, and that had slowly been lengthening in the afternoon sun, finally dropped. And it couldn't have happened at a better moment. Captain Shallcross had just stepped from the door of the engine room. The tar plopped on his shoulder and strung down the back of his silk waistcoat. He grabbed a post supporting the hurricane deck, but as soon as he steadied himself he quickly withdrew his hand and inspected his calfskin glove to see whether it had been soiled by the oily grit that covered almost everything on the boat. In his concern for the glove he had not noticed the tar on his shoulder.

This was good fun, the best thing that could happen as far as the boys were concerned. "Good afternoon, young men," the captain said in his mincing way as he strolled past the boys. Joseph smiled widely at him. The old captain was a pretentious man who wore ruffled shirts and white satin cravats and who obviously thought of himself as very much above the common people traveling on his boat.

"Let's go tell Bill Duggins," Joseph said, not waiting for his brother's response, but running quickly to a nearby ladder and clambering up to the next deck. Matthew followed right behind him. Bill Duggins was the pilot who spent his long days in the wheelhouse carefully maneuvering the steamboat between the shifting sandbars of the treacherous Missouri River. Joseph and Matthew had made friends

1

with him and he let them sit in the wheelhouse sometimes while he told them Indian stories or tales about the river.

"Bill Duggins, you can't imagine what's happened," Joseph said as he leaped through the door. The pilot only glanced at Joseph, then returned his steady gaze to the river ahead. He stood with his heavy legs spread apart, his arms jiggling from the choppy motion of the big steam engine as he slowly turned the wheel. He wore an old red flannel shirt, rolled up to the elbows, and homespun jean trousers. "Captain Shallcross just got tar all down the back of his nice blue waistcoat, but he doesn't know it yet, and he's walking around with it on him."

Duggins took a good look at Joseph this time, and saw Matthew behind him. He grinned and the boys could see where three of his front teeth were missing. "How'd he get himself tarred up?" he asked, with obvious pleasure.

"It was hanging down from the hurricane deck, and finally it dropped off just as he walked under."

"The old goat'll throw a roaring fit when he finally sees it. I'd like to be there when he does."

Just then the captain stepped into the wheelhouse through the door on the opposite side from the boys. "Mr. Duggins," Shallcross said, and Duggins spun around, still grinning. "Mr. Duggins, how long till we reach the Independence landing by your reckoning?"

"Less than an hour, I'd wager. After this big bend, it ain't far at all." Duggins turned back toward the river now; a pilot could never afford to look away from the Missouri for very long. But he had caught a good look at the tar on the captain's shoulder and the boys could see his delight.

"For heaven's sakes, Mr. Duggins, why didn't you say something? Nothing is ready for the landing. The first mate will need to . . ."

"I told him already. He's got the crew working on the riggings."

"Mr. Duggins, when are you ever going to learn that I am the captain of the *Chieftain?*"

2

"Ain't never said you warn't. If you wanna drive her, go ahead." Duggins stepped back from the wheel and motioned to the captain to come over. But Shallcross spun around and walked out the door, the back of his neck glowing red. Duggins glanced back at the boys. "He couldn't take her three mile, and he knows it. He'd have her on a sawyer or run aground on a bar, that's for sure."

"What's a sawyer, Bill?" Joseph asked.

"A snag. A root or a limb or something down under the water where you can't see it. They can rip out the whole botton, sink you on the spot. Some's wrecked that way every single year."

"How can you help hitting one if you can't see it?"

"Well, part's just plain luck, and part's watching real close for them little ripples—see, like them breaks you just make out along by them willows close in by the bank over there. But mostly it's feel. You gotta feel 'em somehow. An old pilot, and a good one, feels 'em."

Matthew had stepped up to look for the ripples Bill Duggins had pointed to. "But how is that possible, sir?" he said. "What do you feel?"

"Don't call *me* sir—save that for Shallcross. I'm just Bill Duggins, pilot. And I don't know about what the feeling is—just something that sorta comes through my arms when I'm at the wheel."

Shallcross was back. "Mr. Duggins, the first mate says that we are going to have to make one more stop to take on firewood. You had better start watching for a decent landing."

"We got plenty of wood, captain, *sir*. I had the boys load on special heavy last time, and they got good dry stuff, even some oak, not just all cottonwood. We'll make her."

"But—" Shallcross began, his face red and his bushy yellow eyebrows pulled together, but he finally said nothing at all.

"We'll make her, Captain, *sir*. You brought her in on time. You sure done a good job."

3

"Never again, Duggins. Never again will you pilot one of my steamers."

"Wasn't planning to."

For a moment the captain's lip quivered and pulled taut against his upper teeth, but he only stood that way for a second or two and then he turned and left again. Bill Duggins chuckled to himself and watched the river. Joseph laughed, but Matthew was still watching the river, and almost as soon as Shallcross was gone, he said, "Mr. Duggins, is that a snag there?"

"Sure is. That's an easy one though. It's almost sticking out of the water. It's them that's a little deeper that can get you." He spit tobacco on the floor to the left of him, wiped his lips on his sleeve, and said, "Matthew, maybe you oughta be a river man. You like the river, don't you?"

"Yes, in a way. It's sort of interesting."

"You two prob'ly getting pretty hot to see your new home now, ain't you?"

"I don't know, Bill," Joseph said. "I'm sort of scared. There might be Indians, and—"

"Injuns ain't nothing to get bothered by. You seen them that was going down river in bull boats—them with the hides. That's how all the Injuns is out here. They don't bother people much. Up river further on it can get a lot worse, but these here ain't doing no scalping."

"Maybe not, Bill, but we're used to living in a house in New York with glass windows and rugs on the floor and nice furniture and all. All we ever see out here are little old cabins and people wearing buckskins. I think I would rather have stayed in New York."

"Why don't you, then?" Duggins spat on the floor again. Matthew was still watching the river, but Joseph stood next to Bill. "Because Father brought us out here, and because the Prophet, Joseph Smith, asked us to come here to build Zion."

"What's that?"

Joseph hesitated and Matthew, after a moment, answered for him.

"It's the place where the Saints will be gathered together before Christ returns to reign upon the earth." Matthew's earnestness reminded Joseph of his father's, and he was proud of Matthew for knowing the answer.

"What's Saints?" Bill Duggins asked.

"It's those who join God's true church, The Church of Jesus Christ of Latter-day Saints."

"I thought you was Mormons."

"That's just what people call us because we believe in the Book of Mormon."

Bill Duggins studied the water for a time and said nothing. Joseph was relieved that he didn't pursue the matter any further. He had found that many people who professed interest in his church seemed to be laughing at the same time. Joseph preferred to be more or less like everyone else, and he feared that Bill Duggins, whom he liked so much, might think him strange.

"Where was it you lived in New York?" Bill finally asked.

"Colesville. Just a little town. Ever hear of it?"

"Nope, but I been in New York before. I used to work canal boats before I came out here."

"We were on a canal boat," Matthew said. "That's how we crossed New York. And then we took a sloop across Lake Erie to Ohio. We stayed there for a while before Joseph Smith called us to come to Missouri."

"We all got sick in that sloop," Joseph said. "We got in a bad storm. Even our father was sick."

"Well, Joseph, I hate to say it, but I'm afeard you ain't seen nothing yet."

"Why, Bill?"

"Your pa ain't no farmer, is he?"

"No, but he says he can farm if he has to."

"Any of your Mormon men farmers?"

"Just a few," Matthew said. "The Knights—Brother Newel Knight is our leader—he and his father and brother had a grist mill in Colesville. Father was a wheelwright. Most all the men had trades, but Father said they are all hardworking men and that they can do anything they have a mind to—with the Lord's help."

"How many of you is going out here?"

"Sixty-two from Colesville. But thousands more will be coming. We are just the first." Matthew, for a boy of twelve, could sound very sure of himself. He was a strong boy, not tall, but sturdy, thick through the legs and chest and shoulders. Built like his father, he had his father's stern gray eyes as well, even his voice and his way of saying things.

"I'll tell you what, boys. I bet you get your wish. I bet you end up back in New York inside a year. I been out here on the Missouri for two year now, since eighteen and twenty-nine in the early part of the year when steamer runs was just getting going regular. I seen lots of folks moving west, and I seen a good many turn 'round and head back too, but I ain't never seen no bunch of Yankees wearing black frock coats in July come out here and try 'n make farmers of themselves. Outside of you Mormons, what kind of folks you seen on this here steamer, boys?"

Joseph answered, "Most of the settlers are from Kentucky."

"That's right," Bill said, "or Virginny, or maybe Tennessee. And they already cleared land before, and already broke sod, and already lived on cornpone and coffee and jerky, and learned how to cure skins to make breeches, and how to hunt, and what to do if the Injuns *should* get bothersome. And the women folk is hard as the men— don't mind hearing some cussing and can shoot a rifle if they have to, and can put in a day in the fields right with their old men. Your women is soft. There ain't no way, boys, there ain't no way you gonna stay out here more'n one winter."

Joseph waited for Matthew to correct Bill Duggins, but Matthew said nothing and Joseph felt the silence take the shape of fear. He looked out across the river. The cotton-wood trees were shedding their cotton and the breeze carried it across the river as thick as snow. It gathered on the

6

water and made the currents discernible. Rather than lightening up the heavy, humid air, it seemed the breeze turned it into gusts from a furnace. Joseph felt the heat more than he had all day; he wiped his forehead with his hand and rubbed the sweat onto his homespun breeches. Sometimes he wished that Joseph Smith had never come along, that his life could have stayed as it had been, or that they could go back to New York and pick up where they had left off. And yet he loved Brother Joseph more than any man he had ever known, more than even Newel Knight, in some ways even more than his—but no, he shouldn't think that—his father was the best of men.

"Don't worry, boys," Bill Duggins said. "Look on the bright side. Won't be long you'll be back East telling the other boys about your big adventure."

"No, sir," Matthew said. "No matter how bad things are, we will never leave. We have been called of God to come here."

"Then I hope he looks out for you, that's all I can say."

Joseph wanted no more of this. "Come on, Matthew," he said. "Let's go find the captain and see if he found the tar yet."

The boys returned to the main deck. There was more activity there than they had seen before. The crew, mostly black men or Irish immigrants, were stirring about, moving cargo. The deck passengers were putting their belongings together, folding up makeshift beds they had slept in under the open sky, and packing trunks or carpetbags. From somewhere a mule skinner could be heard cursing a team of mules he was getting ready to take off the boat at Independence, probably to be used on the Santa Fe Trail, which in the last few years had made Independence a boom town. Trappers were getting their gear assembled. Joseph saw one Kentucky settler still holding the long rifle he had been using throughout the trip, hunting for deer and turkey along the river while the crew loaded firewood, even taking shots from the boat at targets along the shore just to pass the time.

It had been a week now since the Colesville Saints had left St. Louis. They had made good time. The *Chieftain* was dirty and it stunk from the smell of hides, which it often carried, but it was only a year old; it was a solid side-wheeler and had still not been wrecked. Steamers on the Missouri rarely lasted more than three or four years.

The boys spotted the captain talking to the first mate not far from where the crew was carrying firewood to the engine room from the long stack of cut wood on the deck. But as they approached the captain they heard, "Matthew, Joseph," from behind. It was their father's voice. "We will soon be landing, boys; we need to get our things together."

Joseph glanced at Matthew. "Our things are ready, Father."

"Well, that's fine, but you come and watch little Ruth while your mother and I finish packing." Matthew Williams, Sr., was a gentle man in spite of a rather stocky, hard-set look about him. He was not domineering, but he was firm. There was never any doubt that he meant what he said. The boys knew better than to argue, or at least young Matthew did.

"But we want to see the landing," Joseph said, which was true, but not the whole truth. What he wanted most was to be there when Captain Shallcross discovered his disgrace.

His father hesitated and looked at Joseph. In the summer heat he had come out on deck without his dark flannel frock coat, but the stiff white collar stood against his neck, tied with a white cravat. His rich, full beard, black and shiny, covered the knot. Most young men wore only side whiskers these days, leaving full beards to the older generation, but Brother Williams was proud of his heavy beard. He felt that God had blessed man with this protection for the face and that it was vain to fuss with shaving it off each day. "Joseph, you heard me," he said. Then he added, "You may bring Ruth with you when we approach the landing, but you must not let go of her hand for a moment."

8

"Yes, Father," Matthew said. Joseph had turned to look toward Captain Shallcross, who had walked over to the rail and was leaning out to see what lay ahead of the steamer. Brother Williams was prompted by Joseph's glance to look that way too. "For goodness' sake," he said, "the captain seems to have . . ."

"Don't tell him," Joseph blurted out.

"What?"

"I just meant that you wouldn't have to tell him."

"And why should I not?"

"Well, you just wouldn't need to. I mean—he will find out himself, in time."

"What is this, Joseph?" Brother Williams said, but he looked at Matthew, apparently aware that he would more likely get his answer there.

Matthew hesitated and glanced at Joseph. "We saw a string of tar fall on Captain Shallcross, and we just thought . . ." His voice trailed off.

"You thought it good fun to watch him discover it, is that it?"

"Yes, sir." Joseph knew that Matthew would never admit the whole truth—that it was really all Joseph's idea. In fact, Matthew probably already felt pangs of guilt from their enjoying the captain's misfortune. Matthew was simply better than Joseph, and Joseph had always known that. It wasn't just that he was almost twelve and Joseph was only nine. It was something more basic than that. Joseph respected it, but felt little motivation to imitate it.

Nonetheless, Joseph did feel compelled to take some of the pressure off his brother. "But, Father," he said, "the captain is such a—" But his father's quick hand on his shoulder stopped him.

Brother Williams looked sternly at Joseph. To the boy he seemed much more serious than the situation required. They hadn't really done anything wrong, had they?

"Son, listen to me. Captain Shallcross is not what I would call an amicable man. He has not been overly kind to us, nor is he someone whose manner I greatly—how shall I say—respect. He is different. But you must learn that his being different does not justify our being unkind to him. You wanted to laugh at him, at his misfortune, and that is unkind."

"But he always treats us like—"

"Joseph, that is not the point. Now listen. This is something you must understand. I believe God is pleased with us for accepting his gospel, though from the moment we did so we have suffered persecution and insult—in Colesville, in Ohio, even in our travels—and I fear that we must always face this. But we must stand firm against such behavior in ourselves. We must resist the temptation to return hatred with hatred."

Joseph, for the life of him, could see little connection between the fun he wanted to have with Captain Shallcross and all this talk of persecution and hatred. And yet he felt in his father's manner a gravity that was frightening. What hatred, what persecution would they always have to face? Again he felt a wave of homesickness, that same feeling he had experienced a dozen times a day since they had left Colesville in a caravan of wagons—the simple feeling that he would rather not leave, rather not change everything. Sometimes he shuddered to think of the day when the little creek by the Knight mill had been dammed up and his family had been baptized with many of the other Colesville Saints.

To Joseph's surprise his father did not tell the captain about the tar, probably because he preferred to avoid the scene that would follow, but to Joseph it meant that the fun was still available. He just couldn't believe it was all that bad to laugh at old Shallcross. Bill Duggins did all the time.

The boys brought Ruth out on the main deck. This was not really so bad. She was a good-natured little girl, almost three years old. She really didn't trouble them much. Dressed in her best calico dress and a yellow bonnet, she held both boys' hands and toddled along smiling, overjoyed to be with her brothers. The captain was still at

10

the rail, occasionally leaning out to see ahead, but obviously avoiding the wheelhouse, letting Bill Duggins handle the landing.

"Joseph," Matthew said, "remember what Father told us. We shouldn't laugh at the captain."

"I know," Joseph said gravely, but his eyes were wide and ready to deny his voice. Matthew saw this and looked away; Joseph could break through Matthew's gravity with surprising ease. Joseph accepted this much as an affirmation, and he grinned. He had handsome, straight teeth and a wonderfully happy face, gray-blue eyes like his mother's, and a shock of sandy brown hair usually drooping on his forehead. And he had dimples, not deep but quick to appear when his face lighted up.

Some of the Mormon brethren had gathered on the main deck. Hezekiah Peck, Freeborn Demill, and Joseph Knight, Newel's father, were standing not far from the captain. They had donned their coats and silk top hats, as though they felt they had to assume formal dress to step on the blessed land of Zion. In a few minutes word spread that Everrett's ferry was just ahead and the Independence landing only a few minutes beyond. As the boat neared the landing the boys could hear the bells clang from the wheelhouse, and they knew that Bill Duggins was signaling to the engine room the proper power to give the engine. As they floated up to the old log dock the piles creaked and shifted, and a man in buckskins with long hair tied back behind his ears ran from the old log cabin near the dock. "Ease off on her," he cried. "Ye want to run her right over my dock?"

Soon a ramp was set across from the boat to the dock, and the passengers began to carry their provisions to shore, stacking trunks and bedrolls on the ground by the log cabin. Throughout the trip the Mormon travelers had kept largely to themselves and they continued to do so now. Joseph Knight had preached one night to many who had gathered on deck and politely listened, but they were rough-looking people, mostly men. They chuckled a little,

11

even argued a bit with Brother Knight, but after that they just avoided the Mormons and the Mormons avoided them.

Newel Knight brought his old mother, Polly, on deck and helped her slowly across the ramp. Her other son, Joseph Knight, Jr., and Ira Willes followed behind carrying the wooden coffin that Newel had built on the boat after going ashore for lumber one evening. Polly had not been expected to live, but she had prayed for strength, vowing that she would live to see Jackson County, Missouri, the Promised Land. Now she had done it, stood on the land that Joseph Smith had been told in a revelation would be the place of inheritance for the gathering of the Saints.

Joseph stayed with Ruth while Matthew helped their father carry their large trunk off the boat. Bill Duggins came down and tousled Joseph's hair as he walked onto the ramp with his little sister. Finally they were all on land. As they gathered in a group on the shore, everybody stood as though wondering what to do next, aware that they had arrived, full of expectancy, and yet uncertain how to begin. There was no station here, no town, just the rising bluff covered with oaks and heavy underbrush, a dirt road leading away over the bluff toward Independence, the log cabin, and the sound of locusts screaming in unison in the hot July afternoon sun. Joseph longed to see a city, something besides wilderness.

Then Captain Shallcross approached the group, sought out Newel Knight, and shook his hand. Brother Knight was only thirty-one, but he was a good leader, tall, lean, clear-eyed, and full of natural warmth and friendliness. "Well, Captain, you did as you promised—made it by the twenty-fifth, exactly seven days."

"Oh certainly, never a doubt," the captain replied. "You have been excellent passengers. Never heard so little cursing, nor such pious behavior on board one of my vessels."

"Thank you, sir."

"I fear you are deluded in letting Joe Smith convince

you to settle out here on the frontier, but then, that's your matter."

Brother Knight only nodded, but Joseph knew he was resisting a reply. "Thank you for everything," he finally said.

"Yes, sir, and best wishes—" the captain began, but Newel's father interrupted.

"Excuse me, Captain, you seem to have gotten something on you." Everyone had seen it before, and Joseph knew that old Brother Knight was giving in to a temptation.

The captain twisted his head as far as he could and looked from the corners of his eyes. "My goodness! Well, I never. Why . . . I . . . this is the most . . . ruined . . . tar, for heaven's sake . . . I could . . ." He was still stuttering as he walked away, not bothering to say good-bye. "I have never been so . . . my best silk waistcoat . . . however could this have happened?"

Joseph tried not to laugh, but he saw Brother Newel smile just a little and that was too much for him. He broke into a big grin and looked at Matthew, who was staring at his feet battling an urge. Joseph avoided his father's eyes for a long time, grinning with his hand over his mouth, fighting himself mightily. And then he saw that his father was struggling too, even smiling just a bit. In fact, everyone was, and as the captain disappeared some of the brethren even laughed right out loud.

Chapter 2

After a few minutes of discussion, Newel Knight took Benjamin Slade with him and they began the five-mile walk into Independence. Joseph Smith had arrived ahead of the Colesville Saints, and the first order of business was to locate him and see what he had learned about purchasing land. The rest of the Saints carried their provisions a few hundred yards from the landing and set up camp near the bluffs, not far from the river. They had not brought tents, but some of the families had canvas. They built makeshift shelters by cutting cottonwood logs and constructing little V-shaped or three-sided structures just high enough to crawl into. These they draped with canvas or blankets. Others simply slept under the stars where the humid night air settled upon their bedding more like steam than dew.

Joseph lay awake for a long time that night. He wasn't scared exactly, not of Indians or wild animals, but he felt confused and disoriented, empty, even lonely. Being nine, he knew he was too old to move close to his mother or his father, to tell them what he felt, but he couldn't help feeling envious of little Ruth, who lay cuddled close to Mother.

With morning, however, things didn't seem so bad. Breakfast was rather meager, the main course being only corn bread made from crudely ground corn that tasted of the grit from the rock mortar and pestle used to grind it. But after breakfast Matthew and Joseph found the Peck boys, Washington and Mathew, and Clark and George Slade, and the six of them ran through the woods and along the banks of the river, like animals released from captivity. Being off the boat was exhilarating, as was being out of the constant watch of so many adults. It was the boys themselves who first spotted Newel Knight coming up the road on horseback, Joseph Smith by his side.

As the two riders approached, the boys waved and shouted, then gathered around the Prophet's horse as he reined up in front of them. Joseph Smith quickly swung down from the saddle to greet them. He remembered every name, and he talked to each boy briefly but personally, remembering something about each, asking all of them about their trip. He was fairly tall and very muscular. When he shook young Joseph's hand Joseph could feel the strength of the man in the size and grip of his hand. His hair was blond and his eyes blue; he was a handsome man except for his somewhat prominent nose. And he was young, only twenty-six. He looked young too, acted young in many ways, and the boys loved him.

"Little Joseph, how are you? Are you living up to the great name we bear? Are you as righteous as Joseph of old?" Young Joseph didn't answer because he knew the Prophet was teasing him. "Well, I'll take you over my knee if you aren't," he said, and suddenly he grabbed the boy and tossed him up over the horse's saddle like a bag of grain. He gave him three or four whacks across the breeches with mock severity and then pulled him down again, laughing all the while.

Young Joseph was rather out of breath when he came back to the ground, but he laughed with Joseph Smith, looking up at his smiling face. The Prophet had a wonderfully engaging smile, a sort of innocent, boyish grin. Then the Prophet hugged Joseph, pulling him close so that the boy's face nestled against his waistcoat. "I wager I could pull all six of you boys up with a stick. You must all eat better if you want to beat me." One of Joseph Smith's favorite games was pulling sticks, a game in which two contestants sat on the ground facing each other, grasping a stick between them. The winner was the first person to pull the other to his feet. The Prophet had rarely been bested at

15

this, and was even known to have pulled up two strong men at once. Sometimes he would take on the other Mormon men one after the other, using only one hand, laughing as each was defeated. The boys had seen him do it. They believed he could do anything.

Joseph Smith and Newel Knight rode on and the boys ran behind them. When Brother Joseph rode into camp he was immediately surrounded by the Colesville Saints. It amazed young Joseph to see the change come over everyone. The Prophet embraced the men, shook their hands with both of his, grabbed the children up in his arms, drew out the women who stood back, asked a dozen questions. In minutes everyone was laughing, and there were tears in the eyes of many.

And then Polly Knight was brought to the Prophet. Her husband held her around the waist as she told her story—how she had clung to life long enough to arrive in Zion, and how God had granted her this last blessing. Young Joseph saw tears in the Prophet's eyes. A hush fell over the group.

"Brothers and sisters, I promise you that God will bless you for your faith. I know that you have come to a rugged wilderness, but you will see the day when God's great works will be brought to pass here. Others will come after you, but you must pay the greatest price by opening the way for the others. You will have to begin the work of conquering the vast prairie that lies beyond these woods." He spoke softly and everyone strained to hear. "But you have always been the first; you were among the first to accept the message of the restoration of God's church upon the earth. You are some of God's chosen people."

Later Newel Knight explained to the Saints what was happening. Negotiations were underway to purchase land beyond the Big Blue River, near the western border of Missouri where Indian country began. For $1.25 an acre good farmland was available, close to water on the Brush Creek and on the edge of the great prairie. Another plot was available near the Cave Springs. The Prophet had brought some money with him from Kirtland, Ohio, to help the Colesville group get started, but farm tools, wagons, animals, and all else would have to be bought by the people themselves, each according to his ability. A great deal of sharing, both of provisions and money, was going to be necessary. The whole company would have to stand together if they were to survive until the first crops could be brought in. It was nearing August, too late to expect to get much back from the land this season.

Joseph Smith stayed for a few hours, shared the Saints' meager dinner of dried beef, then met with the brethren to discuss further plans. Afterwards he talked with some of the sisters and children. Young Joseph was usually not far away, listening to every word the Prophet said. But he was surprised when the Prophet turned to him and said, "Joseph, let's you and I take a walk down by the river."

The two walked away from the camp toward the bank of the Missouri. When they reached the river Brother Joseph stopped and turned toward the boy. He put his hand on Joseph's shoulder. "Joseph, I suppose I have always taken a liking to you because we share the same name, but today an impression came over me that I have experienced before when I have talked to you. I now recognize it to be a revelation from our Lord, and I think you are old enough to be told. God has made it known to me that you are to be called to a special mission in your life." He stopped to let the idea sink in, but young Joseph could hardly understand what had been said. The very act of being called away for a private talk with the Prophet was so impressive that his mind was in a state of confusion. "You must remain spotless in the eyes of the Lord, Joseph, or you can lose your opportunity."

Joseph nodded, tried to think of something to say, then nodded again. But as the reality of the Prophet's words began to take shape, he felt his throat stiffen. Joseph Smith knelt down in front of him on one knee and looked straight into his eyes. "Don't worry about this. I was called at an early age myself and I understand your concern. Wisdom will come with time, Joseph. For now, learn with a will; be diligent. God will help you prepare yourself, and he will let you know someday what he has in store for you."

Young Joseph nodded again. He felt as though he had taken a deep breath that he couldn't let out. The Prophet stood again and looked toward the river. "Just look how big it is, Joseph, how powerful." Joseph had been watching the river for a whole week, and it had always looked big, but now he felt tiny standing next to it, and next to the Prophet. He was trying desperately to sort out his feelings, but his emotions refused to take the shape of words.

"Well, isn't it?" the Prophet asked. The boy looked at him, confused. "Isn't it big? Isn't it powerful?" And now Joseph could see that Brother Joseph was teasing him. But the boy only nodded, still unable to make any words.

"Joseph, I am afraid I have frightened you. Tell me what you are thinking." The Prophet unbuttoned his waistcoat and took it off. The heat and humidity were rising now in the afternoon sun, and his forehead glistened with sweat.

"I think maybe it would be better if . . ." Joseph stood for a moment looking down at the ground, but then he looked up. "Brother Joseph, I'm not as good as you think. I don't like to listen to sermons and I . . . well, I'm just not very good. My brother Matthew is the one who ought to be called. He's strong and he—"

"Now, Joseph, all I can tell you is what God has made known to me. You will be ready when the time comes. Just trust me, and trust him, Joseph."

"But couldn't you just—"

"Joseph, can you cast a stone across this river?" It took the boy a moment to realize what he had been asked; then he shook his head, not even looking toward the water.

Joseph Smith knelt and found a stone. He stood and looked at the river for a moment and then pulled back his arm and hurled the stone, grunting as he released it. The rock arched a long way out over the river, but when it dropped Joseph was amazed at how close it still seemed. It

18

was nowhere near halfway across. "Neither can I," Joseph Smith said, smiling.

Young Joseph and the Prophet went back then and rejoined the camp. But later on in the afternoon the boy came back to the same place and found a stone. He threw it as hard as he could, but it seemed to travel almost nowhere. It plopped in the water within hearing distance. The Missouri was immense, and to Joseph it seemed big enough to destroy him.

Chapter 3

In a few days land had been purchased and most of the
Saints traveled by flatboat along the Missouri to the Big
Blue River and then down the Big Blue to the land near
Brush Creek. Brother Williams, however, took his two boys
and walked to Independence. He needed tools, ammunition for his rifle, a wagon and a horse, and, if possible, a
cow. His money would have to stretch and he would have
to find some bargains, but he could repair an old wagon if
he had to, and he could get by without a particularly fine
horse. Oxen would have to be purchased too, but the
Saints' plan was to pool the company's money and buy
several teams, and then to share the animals when sod
breaking began.

Joseph had not talked with anyone about what the
Prophet had told him. He told his parents that he had
gone to the river with Brother Joseph and they had thrown
stones in the water—that was all. And he had not really
given much more thought to what the Prophet had said.
Joseph liked to have fun, liked to laugh, liked to be outside.
The very idea of being "called of God" sounded entirely
too serious. If his parents or Newel Knight found out, they
would expect more of him, demand more. He would be
reminded of it constantly. From the moment he had tried
to cast the stone across the Missouri he had said to himself,
"I can't do it, so why should I try?" Someday the Prophet
would realize that Matthew was the one to call. For now
Joseph would just not think about it.

Joseph was surprised by Independence. It was a log-
cabin town, only two of the stores having clapboard siding.
The Prophet had told the Saints that it was like going back

in time one hundred years to enter this place, and now young Joseph could see what he had meant. The homes were crude little cabins with stick and mud chimneys. Chickens scratched in the dust around the cabins, and hogs were penned right next to the houses. Joseph wondered how the people could live with the smell. A dirty little boy was playing by one of the houses, wearing only a shirt that hung to his knees. He turned a dull-eyed face toward Joseph and Matthew and then looked back as his mother walked from the open door of the house. She was a thin woman, all gristle, and was dressed in a buckskin outfit, her sleeves rolled up, showing her rough, reddened arms. When the boy spoke to her she ignored him and disappeared around the corner of the house, leaving the tracks of her bare feet in the dust.

Yet, in spite of its backwardness, Independence was a busy town, busier than Colesville or any other town Joseph had ever seen. In the center of the town square a brick courthouse, two stories high, was being built. The outer structure was completed, but men were working inside. The building was surrounded by tree stumps, the land having been cleared only in recent years. The square was lined with stores on all four sides. Joseph and Matthew followed their father past a blacksmith shop and a store with a sign on the front that read "Lucas and Agnew—Outfitters." Across the way, on the southwest corner, was a big store with the names "Robert Aull and Samuel Owens" printed on the front. This was the biggest store and seemed the busiest; several wagons were lined up in front, with teams of mules standing in the dusty street flipping their ears and sweeping away flies with their tails. There were many people in town, but they were almost all men—men in buckskins for the most part, although Joseph saw one very eastern-looking man in a frock coat and a top hat. An old black man walked behind him, carrying a box. Joseph had seen blacks before, but this was his first look at slavery.

"Listen, boys," Brother Williams said, "why don't you rest there in the city square where I can find you while I see what purchases I can make. Then you can help me load up when I am ready."

Joseph knew that his father did not want them in the stores where so many rough-looking men were about, but that was all right—he would rather look around for himself anyway, without his father's eye on him. Matthew began to walk across the road, which was deeply rutted from times when the dust had been mud. "Let's look around a little, Matthew," Joseph said.

"Father said to wait over here."

"It won't hurt if we just look into some of these stores. Let's just walk once around the square." Joseph didn't wait for an answer but headed for a store on the west side of the square called "McCoy and Lee's." Matthew followed him.

The store was crowded with men—men who smelled bad and who spit tobacco on the floor without even looking for a spittoon. One man, with a long beard streaked with shades of gray, and dressed in buckskin breeches so filthy they were almost black, cussed at the man behind the counter and growled, "I thought I'd saw everything, Bill, but you gone one better. That ain't worth six bits and *you* know it." He was holding a trap of some sort in his hand.

"Now wait a minute, John," the man behind the counter said. "I have to have them brought in from the East and the shipping costs plenty. If you don't want to pay that much, fine, but that's what I gotta have. There's plenty of trappers who pay it and are just glad to get 'em."

The man continued to curse, staring across the counter. "I oughta blow your head off. You're bleeding us dry. It's just plain robbery." His right fist tightened and rose in the air, and for a moment Joseph thought that he was about to hit the store owner, but then the hand came back down flat on the counter. "How much would it be for six of 'em?"

"Let's see. That would be four-fifty."

"Can you give me credit?"

"We don't give credit. You know that, John."

The man stood still and tense. Finally he plunged his hand in his pocket and pulled out two coins, big coins of a

22

type Joseph had never seen. He slapped them on the counter and said, "How many for that?"

The store owner looked at them. "Rightly, it ain't enough for three, but I'll give you three and we'll call 'er square."

"Yeah, and for two bits I'd bust your head open. Then we'd be square."

"Come on, Joseph, let's get out of here." Matthew had been pulling on Joseph's sleeve for some time. "Father wouldn't want us to be here."

The boys walked around the rest of the square, but they didn't enter any more shops. A wagon train was in town, just returned from a trip to Santa Fe. Mule skinners were everywhere. The boys saw two places called hotels, but inside they could hear men shouting and laughing and they knew that these were taverns. Finally they walked to the north side of the new courthouse, where there was a little shade, and sat down on the huge stump of an old sycamore tree.

An hour went by and they grew hot and tired. Once their father had approached them and said that he would not be much longer, but another half hour had gone since then.

Then a barefoot boy came trudging across the road toward them, a boy of perhaps thirteen, but with big arms and shoulders like he was several years older. His buckskin breeches were much too short for him, and his old red flannel shirt was worn through at the elbows. His hair hung in his eyes, but he flipped it back with a jerk of his head as he neared the boys. "How is it you wearing Sunday clothes?" he asked.

The boys were taken rather by surprise, first because he spoke abruptly with the Kentucky twang the boys were still growing used to, but mainly because they were wearing jeans breeches with leather suspenders and homespun shirts. That was hardly Sunday best to them.

"I said how come you got your Sunday clothes on?" He sounded more hostile this time.

"They're not Sunday clothes." Joseph finally spoke up. "We have flannel suits to wear on Sunday."

"Oh you do, do you," the boy said, nodding knowingly, apparently discovering the truth he had suspected all along. "You must be Yankee boys, I take it."

"We're from New York," Joseph said.

"I know who y'are then. My pa talked to your pa, and he says you're coming in here where you got no business 'cause you don't know the first thing about farming. And he says you're Mormons and that Mormons is a bunch of loony Yankees who follow around some loony feller called Joe Smith."

Joseph stood up. "Well, your father is wrong about that," he said. Matthew stood up next to Joseph, but he didn't say anything.

"You better watch yourself, little boy. You're calling my pa a liar. That's a mighty bad thing to do, you know. I'm gonna ask you just once to take that back."

"I didn't say he was a liar. I said he was wrong. Joseph Smith is not—"

"That amounts to the same thing now, don't it? You're still saying what he told me ain't right. You better tell me you're sorry, little boy." He stepped closer to Joseph and doubled up both fists.

Joseph took a half step closer himself and doubled up his own fists. The boy stood head and shoulders over him. "Never mind, Joseph," Matthew said.

But Joseph said, "I think you are the one who needs to say you are sorry. You have no right—" Suddenly the boy's hand lashed out and struck Joseph in the chest, sending Joseph sprawling over the tree stump.

"If you weren't so little I'd—"

And then Matthew hit him square on the jaw. It hardly moved the boy, but it stunned him. He looked at Matthew blankly. Matthew began to flail at him with both fists. The boy took several punches in the face and chest before he could even bring his arms up. He stepped back, but Matthew came at him swinging with all his might. Then finally

24

the boy seemed to realize his situation; he pushed ahead and caught Matthew in a bear hug and the two fell and rolled over in the dirt.

"Get him, Matthew, get him," Joseph was yelling, but the boys were locked in each other's grip, and though they kicked up a good deal of dust, they were doing little damage. A tall man with a huge belly bulging under a buckskin hunting shirt suddenly appeared and lifted the boys straight into the air, Matthew coming loose in the process. The man set the other boy down on his feet and laughed. He had no teeth and his gums shone pink under the dark black stubble of a week-old beard. "What you up to, Ollie? Cain't I even bring you to town once without you finding some little feller to start a-beating on?"

Matthew got up. Joseph was proud to see that Matthew was dirty but not otherwise marked, while at the same time the boy, Ollie, had a swollen lip and a red mark along his right cheekbone.

The man looked at Ollie and started to laugh again, a big heavy laugh from deep inside. "You done 'er this time, Ollie. Looks like you found yourself a wildcat. He got you pretty good, didn't he. These Mormon boys must be made of good stuff."

Ollie started to answer, "But Pa, he never gave me no chance, he just started—" but his pa cut him off by spinning him around and marching him away, one hand at the nape of his neck, laughing all the while and not even saying good-bye to Matthew and Joseph.

Matthew began to brush himself off. Joseph knew he was concerned about what their father would say. "Matthew, you really got him. You won. You got him five or six times right in the face."

Joseph kept praising Matthew but got no response for some time. Matthew seemed more concerned about his clothes. "He shouldn't have pushed you down," he finally said. "He had no right to do that." He sat down on the stump. "But Joseph, you better learn to watch your tongue. You're too big for your own breeches sometimes."

When the boys left Independence that afternoon it was in an old Conestoga-type wagon with no cover. The wagon had barely made it in from Santa Fe; the wood in the box and in the understructure was badly decayed by the heat and the rains of the western trips the wagon had made. Brother Williams said that he would have to rebuild it, but that it would serve their needs. He had bought a mule instead of a horse, and it too had just returned from the long Santa Fe trail. Most of the wagon trains were now using oxen, and mules could be picked up rather cheaply in Independence.

Matthew told his father all about the fight. Joseph was astounded. He had assumed that they would simply not bring it up unless Father somehow had gotten word or had noticed Matthew's dusty clothes.

"Well, Matthew," Father said, "I suppose I don't blame you for wanting to help your brother. But both of you, especially you, Joseph, might have tried to do a little more talking before you started fighting. I know he was trying to start a fight, but you would be surprised what a friendly reply can do sometimes."

"But Father," Joseph said, "he said Joseph Smith was loony and that all of us are loony."

"But he was just trying to make you angry. If you hadn't—"

"He told us that's what his father told him."

Brother Williams nodded. He clucked at the plodding mule, but its big walnut-colored haunches just continued to bulge and sway at the same pace. "Well, that is interesting, Joseph. I talked to his father today—Oliver Markley is his name—and he has a farm over beyond the Big Blue just a mile or so from where we are going to be. He was very helpful—told me where he thought the best farmland was and gave me some advice about farming in this part of the country. He seemed a very kindly man, in his own way. He did say that we were foolish to try our hand at this, not being farmers. I suppose we do seem pretty 'loony' to him."

"Why, Father?" Matthew asked.

26

"Mainly because we have different habits, different manners from most of these people. And then Joseph Smith's story has been told so many times, mixed with outrageous lies. He's been made out to be a villain of the worst order, and a lunatic too. They call the Book of Mormon the 'Golden Bible,' and scoff at the idea that he got it from an angel."

Joseph felt that old dread again. He hated being different, or being thought different. He was no loony and neither was Joseph Smith. If only people would meet the man, listen to him.

"But boys, we cannot fight these people. It is not right to fight them, in the first place, and besides, we would lose."

"But Matthew won. He whipped him."

"Joseph, it is important that you understand this. Matthew lost. So did you. If we let these people teach us their ways, brawling and cursing, then we lose. God sent us here to build Zion, to be a light unto the world, not to learn the wicked ways of the gentiles. God's way is to return hatred with love—and we are called of God."

Chapter 4

Brother Williams had not been able to buy a cow; there had simply not been enough cash. But Sister Williams said they would get by, and surely the next year they could get one. Joseph heard his father say, "We'll have plenty in time, Elizabeth. A log house can be made very nice. We'll put in puncheon floors eventually and glass windows can be bought in St. Louis. Someday we will rejoice to be in this good land."

But for now there was little time for rejoicing. Rude little shelters were set up again and then everyone went to work. Frock coats soon disappeared, and in a few days the men were burned brown by the summer sun. The women worked just as hard; some cooked, others spent their days hewing logs, gathering firewood, looking after the stock, and hauling water from the nearby springs.

Brother Williams was assigned to cut white oak logs for cabins. The boys had a number of chores, including chopping wood, but they spent most of their days helping to strip the logs of limbs after their father felled the trees. Some of the men were beginning the great labor of breaking the sod. Rich, dark soil was gradually turning up from under the deep prairie grass. Several teams of oxen had to be harnessed to a single sheer; the teams would struggle ten or twelve feet before being stopped for men to clear away the sod that had rolled up against the plow. It was slow work and hard, but every day more corn was in the ground, and the Saints hoped for a late frost so a decent harvest could still be brought in. There were deer to be hunted, and wild turkeys, but corn would be needed as their main staple.

Joseph Smith came to camp several times. Some of the other leaders were also in Independence with the Prophet, and twenty-eight elders who had been told to travel to Jackson County, preaching along the way, had begun to arrive. A conference would be held in Zion and then most of the men would return to the East, but some would stay to direct the Church as the immigration continued. Edward Partridge would serve as bishop, and William Phelps and Oliver Cowdery would publish a newspaper. Sidney Gilbert was to set up a store.

Joseph and his family slept beneath a little log shelter chinked with mud and covered with blankets and tree limbs. It was not tall enough to stand up in, but the five of them had room to lie down. Ruth was rather overwhelmed by all the change; she was often cranky and at night she would awaken, crying and frightened. Sister Williams was patient with her, but Joseph felt, though he did not admit it, rather cut off from his mother. He spent much of the day with his father, but Brother Williams was busy, sometimes abrupt, and spent very little time talking with the boys. It was a strenuous time for Joseph, full of work and little fun.

One afternoon, after the camp had been established for several days, a tall thundercloud, billowy and deep gray along the flat underside, rolled in from the southwest. Behind it was a long ridge of blackness that was interrupted sporadically by flashes of lightning. The wind came first, rather suddenly. By the time the first drops began to fall, leaves were being shredded from the trees, and back in the woods a big limb snapped and tore away, finally thudding to the ground. The Saints ran to the one log house that was well underway. There was no roof yet, so people huddled against the south side as best they could and let the rain blow over them. There was not room for everyone—most of the men stood outside under some low redbud trees, away from the tall post oaks and hickories that could possibly be struck by lightning. Rain came in thick waves, the drops as big as snowflakes.

In less than an hour the storm was over, but the prairie grass had been driven flat against the earth, and in the camp all was mud. As the sun returned the humidity was sickening. Joseph had gotten thoroughly soaked. He felt sticky, uncomfortable. It was not long, however, before another wave of thunderclouds advanced and the rain began all over again. The rest of the day and all evening the thunderstorms moved in one after the other. The leaves would stir in the tops of the trees as the sky darkened, and rain would again begin to smack upon the puddles of standing water.

Joseph and his family went to bed early, after Brother Williams tried to patch some leaks in their roof. Joseph slept at first but awoke at a clap of thunder that seemed right inside the shelter with them. His bedding had gradually soaked up water that had either dripped through the roof or run in around the sides of the shelter. He felt cold, tired, miserable—and angry. He began to think of his house in New York again, something he had carefully avoided doing for some days, and as he did it now, tears came. He did not cry aloud—he absolutely would not do that—but he sniffed a time or two.

"Joseph, don't be frightened," he heard his mother whisper. She was next to him, with Ruth on the other side.

"I'm not scared," he said, but his voice caught and he cried more audibly. He wiped his eyes and tried to fight back the tears. "I'm not scared. I'm angry." He bit the words off and they helped him not to cry.

"What are you angry about?" She was leaning on one elbow now. She reached over and ran her fingers across his forehead, brushing his hair to the side. As lightning flashed Joseph could see her face. Her hair, light brown like his own, was pulled back from her face. He could see her eyes reflect the flash of lightning, but there was no flash in the eyes themselves. She was always rather quiet, but now she looked sad. Some of the Saints said she was a plain woman, but she had a lovely, mellow sort of smile that could be very appealing. She did not smile a great deal, however,

30

especially since beginning the trip west. She did not show affection very easily either, and Joseph sometimes longed for more softness from her.

"I'm angry because I'm wet and cold. And I think Ollie was right—Joseph Smith *is* loony." Joseph had never thought to say such a thing, but he wanted to say something angry and harsh. He would like to have sworn, but he didn't dare.

"Joseph, I know you don't mean that," Mother said. She said it with confidence, and Joseph, knowing she was right, didn't contradict her. He saw her face again as the sky brightened for a second. She was not crying. Her face looked firm, rigid. "I don't like it either, Joseph. I'm tired and cold—and I never really wanted to leave Colesville." Joseph had never expected her to say such a thing. There was a slight bitterness, a tightness in her voice. "Your father is more faithful than I am—I came because he was so certain that we should. But I can be strong when I have to be, and you can too, son. Now don't cry. Sleep if you can. It will be morning before long and the sun will return today or tomorrow or sometime, and everything will dry out. And before long we'll have us a house where we can stay warm and dry, and we'll have a nice white fence and a garden, and a cow. . . ." And then she did cry, in spite of herself, and so did Joseph, and she even held him close to her while the thunder rumbled in the northeast as the storm moved away.

The morning did bring sun, drying everything as the afternoon heat began to bake the mud. As evening approached, Joseph Smith and Edward Partridge rode into camp. A treat was cooked for the occasion: fresh venison to eat with the usual corn bread. Joseph had never tasted anything so good.

After supper the Prophet and the new bishop sat for a long time with the Colesville Saints. Joseph liked Bishop Partridge. He was tall and thin, quiet and reserved, just opposite of Joseph Smith, but he too was a warm man who looked in your eyes when he talked to you. Joseph Smith

31

wanted everyone to gather the next day for a ceremony in their camp. The first log would be set in place for a building that would serve as the first school and the first church. "Humble as it will be," the Prophet said, "it will be God's first house in Zion."

Joseph was troubled, however, when he heard the Prophet say that when he had spoken with Mr. Lucas, who owned one of the stores in town, the shopkeeper had expressed concern that more Saints were planning to come to Jackson County. "I told him that it would mean more business and that we could all prosper together, but he only wanted to know how we felt about slavery."

"It's an abomination," old Joseph Knight said.

"Yes, it is, Brother Knight, but we must be careful what we say to these old settlers. Lucas owns slaves, and they cost him plenty, and the same is true of Lilburn Boggs, Sam Owens, and most of the rest of them. They don't want us to come in and tell them what they can do. And, of course, we ought to be able to understand that. They don't really take to us much in the first place, but if we say too much to them about the way they live, they just might think they have the right to tell us to leave. And they outnumber us a long way, Brother Knight."

It was that tone again, the ominous tone Joseph had noticed several times before that seemed to say there was trouble ahead.

"But don't worry, brothers and sisters," Joseph Smith said, and there was that infectious smile of his. "The Lord has great things in store for us here. I see a day when beautiful towns will fill these prairies, and a temple to the most high God will be built here. This is God's land and we are blessed just to set foot on it. God will bless you for what you are doing here, I promise you."

Young Joseph could see the strength of the Prophet's voice flowing into the whole company. There was a simple honesty about Joseph Smith that seemed impossible to reject. If he said that God wanted them to be there, then it was true, and Joseph was sure of that. He felt his mother's

32

arm rest gently on his shoulder, and he remembered with a twinge something he had said one very wet night.

The next day the Saints gathered near the springs and dedicated a spot of land for the school and church. All of the church leaders came, including the missionaries who had arrived. Joseph thought Sidney Rigdon's prayer would never end, but he did find himself enjoying Joseph Smith's sermon. The Prophet told the Saints about Zion as it would someday appear. As Joseph listened he envisioned the town: the brick houses, the temple, the numberless Saints. Everything seemed possible when the Prophet spoke, and the wilderness seemed less threatening. Joseph looked at the hills around the little valley, at the sumac and hazel growing thick along the edges of the woods, which were filled with oaks and hickories and honey locusts. Among these Saints, standing in the tall grass before the church leaders, Joseph felt safe. Maybe this place could become home.

Twelve of the brethren, representing the twelve tribes of Israel, helped to lay a symbolic log. Then Joseph Smith asked the Saints whether they were prepared to live the gospel as they never had before. "We are," they said in unison, their voices not loud but strong. There were no shouts of "Hosanna" or "Praise the Lord," as there sometimes were in church meetings, but there was a sense of resolve that Joseph found reassuring.

Later that day, however, Joseph was disturbed when he heard his parents talking. "Elizabeth, don't misunderstand me," he heard his father say. "I can accept this new law of consecration, and I will. It is from God, through his prophet, and I accept it. I will give freely to the poor and I will give all that we can live without to help the new Saints get started here. And sometime in the future, if we all work hard, we can all prosper. But that is just what bothers me. Not all the brethren work as hard as they could, and I find it difficult to do my share and some of theirs as well. I have always been a man to tend to my own affairs, and I find it difficult to give up my own ways."

"I suppose what bothers me, Matthew," Sister Williams said, "is that some have given so much more to come here than others." Joseph heard something in his mother's voice that surprised him. It was an intensity that bordered on anger; she could be firm, even harsh, but she had never before seemed to lose her control.

"Well now, Elizabeth, we should try to forget that. We had a good business and a nice home, and we gave that up freely to accept God's mission for us. But every man can give what he has, the sweat of his own brow. Maybe some have the health and strength to work harder than others, and I have been blessed with health, and—thank the Lord—I am strong, but every man can do his best. Some of the men just seem to be letting down, though. I know it bothers me more than it ought to. I suppose the Lord will chasten me for my complaining. But I just can't seem to control my anger when I see some of us working so hard and others already slacking off."

"Matthew, what I don't understand is how it can all be made fair. You talked to the Prophet. What does he say? How will it all be made fair? How will it be decided what each family needs?"

"Well, Brother Joseph recognizes there will be some problems, but he says that Bishop Partridge will work this out with each family. When they come here they will consecrate all to the Lord, and they will receive a piece of land for an inheritance. Each family will have to live frugally and give all surplus back to the Church, to be shared with those just beginning. He says that in time everyone will have plenty and that there will be no rich or poor, no petty bickering—a true spirit of brotherhood." Brother Williams was sharpening an ax; as his voice stopped the steady stroking sound continued. Finally he added, "Elizabeth, it's my own selfishness that makes me talk this way. It's Satan's work upon me. I will work from sunrise to sundown and consecrate all to the Lord. It's the weakness of my flesh that makes me speak this way about my brothers."

Joseph was astounded at the idea that his father could

be weak, that Satan could work upon him. Obviously life was much more complicated than he had ever realized, and it seemed to get more so every day.

Chapter 5

The next morning began hot and humid and got steadily worse. By noon it was so insufferable that the men took two hours for lunch, some of them sleeping in the shade and others walking to the spring to cool their feet. Everyone was feeling the heat. Two log houses were nearing completion, but almost everyone was still sleeping in tents and shelters, and this also was becoming tiresome. Polly Knight was weakening fast and everyone said that she couldn't last much longer. After the joy of the meeting the day before, people were surprisingly cranky under the pressure of the oppressive heat. Levi Hall even raised his voice to Newel Knight when Brother Knight told him that it was not proper to strip to the waist to work, not even in the fields away from the sisters. And the sisters too, with complaining children to contend with and so much work to do, became less sisterly in some of their responses to each other. Joseph even thought he heard one sister swear under her breath when her thumb slipped and rubbed across a washboard, though he was certain that she wouldn't do such a thing.

But for Joseph and Matthew the heat became a benefit: Brother Williams told them to take the afternoon off to take a swim. They had been wishing for time to hike down to the Santa Fe trail to see whether any wagon trains were coming through—sometimes they could hear the mule skinners barking at their teams in the distance—but this was no day for hiking. They took their father's advice and headed for the spring. After a splash in the pond, they decided to build a little dam in the small creek that flowed from the springs into the woods. This would give them a shady, private place to swim, maybe a hole deep enough to dive into. They set about working with more enthusiasm than they ever seemed to have for real work.

Since the day Joseph had spoken with Joseph Smith he had been trying not to think about what the Prophet had told him. But now he was gradually having more trouble pushing the thought out of his mind, so he decided to tell Matthew, just to relieve himself of some of the burden. They had both rolled up their trousers and were walking in and out of the water, carrying rocks and sticks that they tried to pack together with the red mud from the creek bank. As Joseph recounted what had been said, however, they began to work more deliberately to avoid making so much noise.

When Joseph finished, Matthew said, "It's a fine thing, Joseph. You will be a great man someday." Matthew was standing in the water by the row of stones they had piled up. Joseph sloshed into the water toward him.

"Not as great as you, Matthew. I'll wager you have a greater mission than me."

"Joseph Smith never told me so."

"That doesn't mean you won't. You are better than me, Matthew; in every way, you are. Someday you will be a leader like Bishop Partridge or Brother Knight, maybe even like Joseph Smith. You can probably already throw a stone farther than any boy in our camp."

"You don't become a leader by throwing rocks, Joseph."

"I know. But leaders are strong. And you're strong, Matthew."

"But Joseph, I don't want to be a leader. I just want to be a good worker like Father. I don't like to give speeches and worry about what everyone is doing."

"I don't either, Matthew," Joseph said. "I hate speeches. I think I'll be like Father too."

Matthew had carried a heavy slab of sandstone to the creek. He placed it against the rocks, inside the dam, to bolster its strength. "You can't help it, Joseph," he said as he looked up. "You have been called of God. You will have to do it."

Joseph and Matthew faced each other standing in the creek, water rippling against the calves of their legs. They were as unlike as brothers could be. Joseph was going to be tall and thin, and he was the color of the river sand from head to foot. Matthew was solid as a stone and his hair was the color of the earth turned up from under the deep prairie grass. "Matthew," Joseph said, "please don't say that any more. Let's not talk about it. It makes me scared. If you will be the great one, I will be like Hyrum Smith is to Joseph Smith. I'll help you."

"But the Lord called Joseph, and he is the younger brother, like you," Matthew said.

They went on with their work then, rather silently. Joseph still refused to think much about what the call would mean, but he felt deflated, as if the world had dropped a great and serious weight upon his back. He had wanted Matthew to take some of this burden, but Matthew had only given it back to him.

After about half an hour Joseph looked up from the dam, which now had begun to create a bit of a pool, maybe two feet deep, and saw something red coming through the trees. It was a man in a red shirt, he thought at first; then he recognized the boy they had fought in town, Ollie. He was wearing the same red shirt, only dirtier, and he had on a straw hat with a big brim that was coming unwoven on one side.

Ollie stopped at the bank and looked at the brothers, who stood side by side, expectantly. "So it's you two. I was hoping I'd run into you two some time. You ready to finish that fight we had going in town?"

"We don't want to fight you," Matthew said. "We never did."

"You hit me before I was ready that last time. But now I'm ready. Come on." He doubled up his fists and crouched over.

"I have no reason to fight you, Ollie," Matthew

answered. "I only did before because you pushed my brother down."

"If that's what it takes I can do it again." Ollie lumbered into the water and reached for Joseph. Joseph instinctively drew back, and when Ollie pushed him he was already falling into the water. He sprang back up, wet, but unhurt.

"Leave him alone," Matthew said, grabbing Ollie by the left arm. With amazing swiftness Ollie's right hand shot up and cracked Matthew across the cheek, dropping him in the water on his backside. Matthew scrambled up into waiting fists. He took two thudding blows to the sides of his lowered head and went down again, this time on his hands and knees. Then Ollie kicked him in the neck and collarbone with the shin of his leg catching him just as he was trying to get up again and flipping him over on his side in the water.

As Ollie strode toward Matthew, Joseph suddenly was on his back, squeezing his head with one arm and hitting him in the ear with the other. Ollie slipped and fell, reaching out to catch himself, but Joseph retained his hold and hit him again and again. After a moment of furious thrashing, Ollie slipped from Joseph's headlock and quickly stood up. He sloshed his way onto the bank, turned, and faced the two boys, both in the water, both down. "All right. Come on. Both of you. I can lick the two of you. Is that what you want?"

Joseph stood up, crouching and ready to attack. But Matthew was still down on his knees, holding his shoulder and letting his arm hang to his side. Joseph said, "Come on, Matthew," but Matthew only shook his head. "You hurt my brother," Joseph yelled, darting toward Ollie. Ollie caught him easily and shoved him back. Joseph went over backwards, splashing in the water, but in one motion he was already turning over and scrambling back up. He tried to come at Ollie low this time, to get him around the legs, but Ollie caught him again, pulled him up, and shoved him back in the water. Almost as quickly Joseph was coming back up, but this time Matthew got there first. He took a wild swing at Ollie's head, missed, caught a blow from Ollie on the mouth, and dropped to his knees. He grabbed Ollie and tried to get up, but he took three quick blows in the face as Ollie stepped back—left, right, left— and down he went again.

"You had enough?" Ollie shouted. But Matthew reached out and caught Ollie by the ankles and with a quick motion flipped him on his back. Ollie grunted as he thudded against the ground, then moaned and lay still.

All three remained silent. Joseph stood looking down at Ollie, but Ollie's eyes seemed distant as though he had been dazed. One eye was already puffing up. Matthew looked much worse: one side of his face was red, the eyelid fluttering and beginning to swell, and blood was running from his bottom lip. But he got to his feet.

"Are you all right?" Matthew said, looking down at Ollie.

Ollie groaned but didn't say anything. Matthew and Joseph knelt down by his head, one on each side. "Ollie?" Joseph said.

"My back hurts," Ollie finally said. "You dropped me square on a rock."

Joseph grinned. But Matthew didn't. "I'm sorry," Matthew said, much to Joseph's surprise.

And then to his even greater surprise, Ollie said, "Ah, that's all right." He sat up. "Pretty good fight, huh?"

They all agreed it was. In fact, within a few minutes Joseph even began to take some pride in it. It made him feel rather grown-up to have been in a "pretty good fight" with a big fellow like Ollie.

Ollie wanted to know what they were making. They told him they were building a dam and asked him if he wanted to help. At first he said he didn't, but when the boys went back to work on it he soon joined them. Matthew washed his face in the cool water several times, but his eye gradually went shut. One of Joseph's eyes looked a little swollen too. But for the time being they didn't worry about that. They gradually got enough of a dam built to back up a fairly nice little pool, if not a very deep one. They talked about felling trees and bringing in bigger rocks, building a tall wall that would create a pool deep enough to dive into. Ollie said he had watched beavers build dams, and he knew just how to do it. They agreed that if their fathers would let them have some time away from work on Saturday they would come back and work some more on the dam. Ollie wanted to work on Sunday, when he said his father let him have most of the day off, but the boys said they would never be allowed to come to the spring on the Sabbath.

"What's the Sabbath?" Ollie wanted to know.

"Sunday. When you go to church," Joseph said. "Don't you go to church?"

"Naw," Ollie said. "Me and Pa usually hunt or fish—or else he goes into town and gets drunk and lets me do what I want."

"What does your mother do?" Joseph wanted to know.

"I ain't got one. She died when I was real little. I can't even remember her."

As they parted and said good-bye to Ollie, Matthew and Joseph were in good spirits, but as they approached the camp Joseph began to wonder what his parents would say. Their mother saw them coming first, took a second look, and let out a cry. In a few minutes Joseph and Matthew were rehearsing their tale of battle before their father and after that before several more of the brethren. At supper they told the whole thing again, while the entire camp listened. Joseph did most of the talking, and he made Matthew out to be quite a hero—David finally bringing down the mighty Goliath. The men obviously enjoyed the story; even Brother Newel laughed when Joseph told how he had jumped on Ollie's back. He admonished them to avoid such dangerous situations, but he seemed to take it rather lightly.

But their father did not, and he told them so after supper. "You boys know what I think of fighting. I thought we had that settled." Joseph could see a serious talk coming.

"But we couldn't help it," Joseph said. "He started it."

"No one ever has to fight. Nothing is ever settled by it. It only—"

"But Father, we made friends after. He's going to help us build the dam."

"Joseph, that is not the point. Fighting is wrong; it's Satan's way. What did I tell you when you fought that boy the first time? If we start to take on the ways of these people here, brawling and swearing and blaspheming, then Satan will have his victory. We are Christians, not heathens."

"But Father, we—"

"Joseph, I do not want to discuss this any further. We have been called of God to build Zion. We must think of that every day of our lives. We are not ordinary people."

That was the worst thing he could have said, as far as Joseph was concerned. Joseph hated more than almost anything else the thought of being unordinary.

Chapter 6

On the fourth of August a conference was held at the home of Joshua Lewis, not far from where the Colesville Saints had begun to establish themselves. Brother Lewis had been converted by Parley P. Pratt and the other missionaries who had first come to Jackson County in 1830. Joseph Smith told those who attended the conference that he, along with seven other leaders, had dedicated a spot of land near Independence where a great temple would someday be built. The dedicated land would have to be purchased and the Saints would have to plan for this great undertaking. It was a long day, very hot, and Joseph suffered as he sat and listened to the sermons, the discussions, and the hymns of praise. He slept through most of the afternoon session.

Two days later Polly Knight finally died. Joseph Smith came to the Colesville Branch on the seventh of August and delivered a beautiful sermon. Afterwards he bade the gathered Saints farewell, told them he was leaving within a day or two to return to Kirtland, Ohio. Word came back two days later that Joseph Smith and Sidney Rigdon and some of the elders had left in canoes to travel down the Missouri. Joseph felt a terrible loneliness set in, more than he had felt for some time, and he knew that a very long winter was ahead.

The weather remained hot until late August when one night, without warning, an early frost struck. It was not heavy, but it did some damage to the corn. The Saints had prayed for a late frost—Joseph had heard them several times at evening prayers—and yet the first frost was earlier than any that the old settlers had ever seen or heard of before. To Joseph it seemed a bad omen. Everyone said that God was going to give them special care in Zion; how could he begin by taking some of the corn away, the little bit of corn they had found time to plant?

After the frost the fall colors set in quickly. The sumac turned a brilliant deep red along with the grape vines that clung to the trunks and limbs of the trees in the oak forests. As the elms yellowed along with the hickory, and the oaks changed to shades of red and bronze, and as the heat passed away, Joseph did begin to feel a growing sense that this was not such a bad place. There were a few red maples across a stretch of prairie about a quarter of a mile from camp. They turned red-orange at the tops and then gradually shaded into deeper reds. Joseph liked to sit in the afternoon sun when the light angled against the trees, highlighting them, and think about the maples near his home in New York. He began to feel less sadness in the memory.

These were the "smoky days," as the old settlers called them, when the Indians would burn the prairies over in Indian country, hunting the fleeing animals, stocking up for winter. It seemed adventurous to Joseph to be so close to Indians even though he had grown used to seeing them pass by the camp, sometimes stopping at the springs. He was growing increasingly confident that the Saints could live here. He had seen what the brethren could do. In fact, by mid-September he had moved into a house, a little one-room cabin with dirt floors and a loft for the children to sleep in. But it was comfortable, warm when the fire was burning. The men were becoming better hunters and there was plenty of fresh meat. The corn bread was still very coarse, but Brother Knight was to build a mill the next spring, and Joseph would have felt still better if the Lord had provided a fine harvest of corn. Everyone said that there would still be enough if they were careful, but Joseph wanted to know that God would help. If he was called of God, as Joseph Smith said—and he couldn't help but think about this from time to time—he was going to need help.

44

Late in the summer more Mormons began to arrive. Another group, led by Peter Whitmer and known as the Whitmer settlement, established themselves near Brush Creek, just a couple of miles from the Colesville Saints. The Rockwell family built a cabin near the Big Blue River and began to operate a ferry. Parley P. Pratt came to the Colesville Saints and agreed to live with them that winter and teach the school. Thomas Marsh and his family also joined the group that fall. About three hundred Mormons had arrived before winter set in.

School opened as soon as the cold weather began. Houses were still being raised, and whenever everything was prepared and logs were cut and hewn, school would be let out and a cabin would go up in one day. These were fun days, with plenty of food and a good deal of time for the boys to play when their help wasn't needed. Since more families had joined the Colesville settlement, it was impossible to finish enough houses for everyone before hard frost, so several families lived in the big cabin together.

Several times during the fall Ollie came to the springs to meet Joseph and Matthew, and they worked on their dam. It was too late in the year to swim or even to wade in the water as they worked, but they were able to gradually create a strong dam, if not a very deep swimming hole. As enthusiasm for the dam dwindled, however, interest in a cave they found nearby began to grow. They wanted to explore it, assuming that no one ever had. Ollie promised to bring a bear-oil lantern someday, if he could get one, and they would become explorers. Joseph and Matthew enjoyed talking about it, but they never expected it to happen. Then one Saturday morning Ollie showed up at their cabin. He stood outside and whistled. When the boys came out he was standing there with the lantern. "Come on. Hurry. I got a light, but I gotta get it back soon. My old man don't know I got it."

The boys got permission to go to the springs. For a dreadful moment Joseph thought Matthew was going to tell the whole truth, that they wanted to explore a cave, but he didn't. Permission was granted, so long as the wood chopping was done before the day was over.

They ran to the cave, but they entered slowly. The smell of bear grease in the lantern was strong, but they could still smell the musty rottenness of the cave. A trickle of water echoed from deep in the darkness somewhere. Ollie moved slowly ahead and the boys followed, Joseph peeking around Ollie to see what lay ahead. The cave narrowed abruptly after twenty feet or so, then curved to the right. It eventually became low enough that the boys had to stoop to walk. Joseph and Matthew had begun to wear boots again now that the weather was cold, and even though Joseph's were last year's boots and hurt his feet, he was glad to have them. Ollie was barefoot as always and Joseph knew that his feet must be freezing. Joseph also wondered about bats, but he said nothing.

"Ollie," Matthew said, "I don't think we should go back in too far. If the lantern should go out . . ."

"Don't be a coward," Ollie said. "If you're scared, go on back to your mama."

Matthew didn't answer, and they continued on to a place where the cave opened up into a larger cavern. The trickle turned out to be a little rivulet that dribbled into a shallow pool. There were even some rusty-looking limestone formations along the top and on one side of the cavern. Eventually the pool covered most of the floor of the cave, but the boys continued through it until they came to a point where everything stopped, except that Ollie found a hole at the base of the wall just big enough to crawl through. It was partially filled with water, perhaps six inches deep.

"Wanna try to go on through?" Ollie asked.

It sounded unthinkable, but Joseph said, "Do you?"

"Naw, I guess not. I'm prob'ly too big. A little feller like you could do it, though. Here, take my lantern."

Joseph could see Ollie grin, his teeth and eyes yellow in the lantern light. Joseph took the lantern, mainly to call Ollie's bluff. He bent and peered back into the low passage. It actually appeared to open up again after a few feet, but Joseph said, "It just stops a little way back there. You can't get through." Joseph was lying, but mainly for fun, to win his game with Ollie.

"You wouldn'a gone anyhow, would you, Joseph? Now tell the truth."

Joseph only smiled, but Matthew said, "Don't put it past him; Joseph will try anything. Except I would have stopped him."

The boys stood in the cold pool for a moment, and Joseph could feel the water seeping into his woolen socks, but he didn't want to turn around and go back. They were at the end already and the whole adventure had only taken them seventy or eighty yards from the cave entrance. "Well," Joseph said, "at least we have a good hideout in case we ever need one."

"What you need to hide from, Joseph? You planning to be a holdup man or something?" Ollie's voice echoed hollowly back at them. He walked out of the pool, back to the place where they had entered the cavern. But instead of leaving, he sat down on the floor of the cave and leaned his back against the wall. Joseph and Matthew followed him; Joseph sat down next to Ollie, but Matthew remained standing.

"If we ever have trouble with the Indians we could hide up here," Joseph said.

"Injuns! Joseph, why're you always talking about Injuns? Them old Delawares and Pottawatamies that comes through here on their way to Injun country ain't got no fight left in 'em."

"My pa says they're Lamanites and they used to be a great people and someday they are going to join our church and become great people again."

"That's the kind of talk that makes my pa burning mad. He says the Mormons is looking for trouble if they keep talking about making friends with Injuns and niggers. He says that Mormons is all Yankee fools and wants to turn all the slaves loose."

"Of course we do. Slavery ain't right—*isn't* right."

Ollie laughed suddenly and the first crack of his loud voice bounced around in the cavern. "What'sa matter, Joseph? You afraid to say *ain't?* That's just the problem with your kind. You always think you have to be fancier than other folk. That's how come folks round here don't like you."

"There's nothing wrong with talking right. Is there, Matthew?"

Matthew stood silent for a moment, in the shadow away from the lantern. "No," he said. "Our father gets angry with us if he hears us using bad grammar. He says it's a sign of ignorance."

The cave was silent. Joseph heard the trickle of water again. He knew Matthew had said the wrong thing. Joseph could only see part of Ollie's face, but he had never seen him look so serious. The shadow from the lantern hid his eyes, but Joseph could see his jaw set, the muscle by his ear swollen and tight. Joseph didn't want this; he liked Ollie. Ollie was stronger than any boy he had ever known. He could throw a rock almost as far as Joseph Smith could, and he could run forever without stopping. He wasn't ignorant either. He knew the names of every kind of tree, and could recognize what tribe an Indian belonged to just by looking at him. He could make calls like any kind of bird. He was big and, in a way, slow, but he was powerful and confident. Joseph trusted him, believed in him.

"Ollie," Joseph said, "if you wanted to, maybe I could talk to my pa and to our teacher and maybe you could go to our school with us."

Ollie's head jerked around. "I don't want nothing to do with your ol' school, Joseph."

Silence again. Joseph had known even as he had said it that it was the wrong thing to say. But the idea of having Ollie at school seemed excellent to Joseph. School would be better with Ollie there—and Ollie did seem to lack a few refinements that even Joseph was willing to admit. "I just meant . . ."

48

"I told you, Joseph, and I don't want to talk no more about it. I don't need to dress up in no fancy-Dan clothes and sit around and listen to no big-shot teacher all day. You two'd be better off if you didn't either. You're both trying to be big-shots yourselves."

"No we ain't, Ollie. We ain't." Joseph spit on the ground between his boots. "School ain't that bad. It surely ain't. Honest, Ollie, you'd like it."

Ollie looked at Joseph and shook his head. "Hang it, Joseph, you don't even know how to say 'ain't' right, and you can't even spit right neither."

"I can say 'ain't' durn near as good as you, Ollie."

"Joseph!" Matthew said, shocked at both his brother's use of bad grammar and his cursing.

"I can too!"

"If I tell Father you can just . . ."

"Leave him alone, Matthew," Ollie said, as he got to his feet. "At least Joseph is trying to be a regular feller, even if he don't know how yet. That's more than you can do."

"Come on, Joseph. Let's go," Matthew said.

"No sir," Joseph said. "I ain't leaving this cave till I feel like it."

"Joseph, you come with me," Matthew said.

"I told you to leave him be, Matthew," Ollie said. "You can't make him do nothing. Me and Joseph can leave when we get ready to. We got the lantern. You go ahead if you want. I think old Joseph is going to turn out to be a mighty good feller, but you never will."

"You don't understand, Ollie," Matthew said. "You can't understand. Joseph is not just any boy. He has been called of God for a special mission. He's no heathen."

"Matthew, why do you have to—" Joseph began to speak, but Ollie's voice drowned his.

"Is that what I am, Matthew? A heathen?"

"Not exactly. I didn't mean that." His voice trailed off timidly. "But you shouldn't curse and swear and you shouldn't teach bad things to Joseph."

"Matthew, I can take care of myself," Joseph said with a hostility that surprised even himself. "Me and Ollie can say anything we want. You're just a coward, that's what I think."

"Yeah, Matthew," Ollie put in, "you better get out of this dark cave before the lantern goes out and you have to cry for your mama."

Matthew stood facing the other two, his face just barely visible as the lantern flickered shadows around him. "Joseph," he finally said, "you know what's right. Come with me. We better go."

Joseph had never been caught in such a trap. As Matthew had stood there silently, even nobly, Joseph had begun to regret what he had said, but he hated to lose face in front of Ollie now. "I'll come when I get ready," he said, but his voice lacked its former power.

"Come *now*," Matthew said, exactly as his father would have, and he turned and walked confidently into the dark. Joseph stood by Ollie for a few seconds, listening to the steady tread of Matthew's boots on the cave floor. "Well," he said, "I guess I better go." Ollie walked ahead and Joseph followed.

Outside Matthew was waiting. When the other two appeared, he turned and walked toward the path leading home. Joseph let Matthew walk a ways, then turned to Ollie. "Come next Saturday and we'll try to find another cave to explore, all right?"

"Maybe, " Ollie said. "Prob'ly not." He walked away in another direction.

Joseph followed Matthew home, but he stayed behind. As they approached their house, however, Matthew stopped and let Joseph catch up. He stood waiting, his broad jaw set and his eyes firm. He looked very old to Joseph—too old. "Joseph, how can you talk that way?" He stared at Joseph and waited, but there was no answer. Joseph didn't hang his head, but he didn't look Matthew in the eye either. "Joseph, I will agree not to tell Father if you promise never to curse again."

Joseph still didn't answer, just stared straight ahead. Then Matthew's face softened. "Joseph, how can you forget what the Prophet told you? You just can't act like the gentiles do."

"Ollie ain't bad," Joseph said, but his voice was not fierce, not even strong. His stubbornness was persisting now.

"I'm not saying he is. But you know what I mean. You have been chosen by the Lord, Joseph, chosen by the Lord. You cannot forget that for a single day, a single minute. You cannot be common, Joseph. You cannot give way to the sins of these common people."

"I wish He had chosen you," Joseph said. "I don't want to be called." He didn't tell Matthew he was sorry and he didn't promise not to swear again, but he had given in and he knew it, and he knew Matthew knew it. But he did wish, as he wished every day, that Matthew had been the chosen one. Matthew was big and strong, bigger than Ollie in his way, and Joseph knew it.

Chapter 7

Joseph and Matthew didn't see Ollie again that fall, and then winter set in and they hardly saw anyone except the Colesville Saints. On Sundays they met in the school to hear Newel Knight or one of the other brothers preach. Meetings sometimes lasted for hours, and Joseph chafed at the tediousness of those Sabbath days. No playing was allowed; and Joseph was even told to repent when he talked or laughed too loudly.

The boys spent most of their days in school. When a blizzard set in there was no school, but the boys studied at home under their father's supervision. Usually Joseph was glad to get back to Brother Pratt's teaching after a day or two with Brother Williams; Father expected much more of the boys and had little patience with their errors. Brother Pratt was demanding too, but he dealt gently with his students. He was a stern-looking man with strong features and a commanding tone of voice, but his manner with the children was almost never harsh. He had been with the first missionaries to come to the land of Zion the winter before, and Joseph loved to hear him tell about the terrible winter of 1830-31 when all Missouri had been covered with three feet of snow and Brother Pratt had hiked from St. Louis to Independence and on into Indian country. Joseph knew as he listened that he was in the presence of one of the great men of the Lord's church; somehow it consoled him to know that he could never be as great as Parley Pratt. His inferiority to such a man of faith was the best evidence Joseph had to convince himself that he would never be called to do anything particularly important, in spite of what the Prophet said.

After school the boys were expected to complete their lessons. Father did most of the wood chopping now, since he had little else to do. But he did keep his promise to Mother and put down a puncheon floor in the cabin. In the evenings the family sat around the fire while Father read aloud from the Bible or the Book of Mormon. Joseph rarely listened; he just sat quietly as Father demanded, pretending to be taking it all in. Sometimes Father asked questions, and when he could prove that Joseph had not been paying attention, a stern reprimand would follow. Still, for the life of him Joseph could not become interested. Matthew, on the other hand, usually answered Father's questions, proving to Joseph's satisfaction that Matthew really was the one with a destined mission.

Some evenings the family talked and laughed, played with Ruth, or baked apples by the fire. They had only two crudely made chairs, so the children sat on the floor near the fire. The smell of the apples was delicious and the light and warmth of the fire were comforting. At those times Joseph felt that his family had found a new home, that all was well.

Joseph did worry about his mother at times. She seemed to have become more quiet, more subdued than he had known her to be before, and he sometimes remembered the night of the rainstorm when she had told him that she didn't want to be there, but that she could be strong. Joseph wondered how strong she was; she didn't look strong to him, and she didn't look happy.

At night the boys climbed a ladder to a loft and slept on straw-filled mattresses on the floor. Ruth slept by her parents' bed in a little crib Father had built. The house was fairly tight and near the fire it was always adequately warm; however, in the loft it could get extremely cold. The straw beds were plenty warm, but getting up in the morning was difficult.

Some of the Saints were very crowded, with more than one family in a cabin—in that regard the Williamses were fortunate—but everything seemed to go well enough. The

53

food was holding out and the winter, so far, had not been a severe one. But in December some of the children were taken ill with a fever, and within a week or two almost everyone in the camp was sick. Perhaps no one came closer to dying than Parley Pratt; he continued very ill for several weeks and was sometimes delirious for days at a time. At first other brethren took the school in charge, but after a time too many were sick and school was closed. In the big cabin that so many shared virtually everyone was sick, with the stronger ones nursing the others as well as they could. Father had gone at first to help, but after a few days he fell sick himself. He brought the illness home and soon all the children had it.

Matthew was much worse than anyone else. He vomited until he was exhausted, tried again and again to hold some food down, but only vomited everything he ate or drank. Finally his fever went so high that his whole body was ablaze. Mother carried snow from outside and rubbed it on his face and head, desperately trying to relieve him, but Father, from his bed, admonished his wife that she would kill him, that the fever had to break, that Matthew must be wrapped in wool blankets. Joseph watched his mother pretend to wrap Matthew in the blankets to satisfy Father, but she could not bear to add to Matthew's discomfort and Joseph knew that. He wondered who was right. Would Matthew die? He thought of little else for several days as he watched Matthew roll on his bedding, which had been brought downstairs. Joseph vomited too, and he had a high fever, but it was nothing like Matthew's. His discomfort only taught him how much worse Matthew's was.

But Matthew recovered, and so did Joseph, Ruth, and Father. In fact, no one in the camp died, and the Saints counted it as a great miracle, a blessing of the Lord. Their spirits were very high as everyone finally recovered; they praised God in their meetings. Some even spoke in tongues. Even young people, Joseph and Matthew's age, stood and gave testimony that the Lord had spared them. But Joseph wondered, as he always did. Why did it have to happen at all? Why did Matthew have to suffer so? Father said that it made them stronger, more united—that it was a blessing. Joseph wondered. And through it all Mother was never sick, or at least she said she never was. But she grew thinner, and she looked tired, and when it was all over Joseph felt that she had lost more than anyone else in the family, that she had recovered less.

The best day of the winter came on February 2, when Orrin Porter Rockwell got married. It was the first marriage among the Mormons in Zion, and all the Saints gathered at the Rockwell ferry at the mouth of the Big Blue to celebrate not only the marriage but also the coming spring and the success expected in the first full growing season. The weather cooperated, the day being unseasonably warm and fine. Porter Rockwell was a shy boy, just eighteen; he walked with a limp from a badly broken leg he had received in his childhood. He was Joseph Smith's cousin and no one loved the Prophet more. Luana Beebe, a daughter of a Mormon family that had settled near Independence, became Porter's wife. The day brought a reunion of all the Saints from all the settlements, and to Joseph it was most exciting. He met half a dozen new boys his age; he wrestled with them and pulled sticks, and he told about his swimming hole. Some of the boys had brought willow fishing poles and they tried to catch fish in the Big Blue. Giving that up after a while, they tried to see who could throw a stone the farthest. Joseph lost at everything—he was smaller than most and lighter than any of them—but no one tried harder, strained harder, threw harder. And no one accepted defeat more good-naturedly. The other boys liked Joseph; he could tell that, and he liked them in return. Before the day was over they turned to him increasingly to lead the way, to think what to do next. There was plenty of good food (fresh venison and turkey) and fiddle music and talk, and very little sternness. Best of all, though there were some speeches, there was no preaching, or very little, and that was just the way Joseph liked it. Matthew had gone his separate way with older boys, and even that pleased Joseph. He enjoyed the freedom and the newfound authority he felt with other boys.

Winter set back in after that day, and then spring began with heavy rains, delaying plowing. Brother Pratt left on a mission, but other brethren kept the school going. It was late April when spring finally mellowed; by then Joseph was as happy as the blue jays to feel the return of warmth. School was let out so the boys could help with the spring plowing and planting, and that too was fine with Joseph.

In April word began to spread that Joseph Smith was coming to Jackson County again and that he planned to hold a conference for all the Saints in Zion. Several times Joseph heard the adults in the Colesville settlement refer to the need for the Prophet to come, the problems that had to be solved. He wondered what problems they were referring to. Once he heard his father whispering to his mother as they sat outside early in the evening. Joseph could not hear all that Father said, but he did hear that several families had refused to accept the law of consecration, and some had even decided to leave Zion and reject the Church. And he heard that Joseph Smith and Sidney Rigdon had written to Bishop Partridge and William Phelps and admonished them to repent.

"Whatever could he mean?" Mother said.

"He said that he recognized a complaining spirit in them."

"Not in Bishop Partridge! How could he say such a thing?"

"Well, Elizabeth, I think the Prophet needs to come here and see. He doesn't understand some of our problems. He really ought to stay here, you know. This is Zion, and I cannot see why he wants to stay in Ohio when the great work is taking place here."

Joseph had never heard his father criticize the Prophet. It shocked him—it angered him. Joseph's love for the

Prophet was fierce. He felt confident that his father was wrong, that the Prophet knew what was best. He wanted to call his father to repentance, just the way his father did when Joseph was unrighteous. At the same time, he also hoped that the day would soon come when Joseph Smith would stay in Jackson County. Nothing could strengthen the Saints more, and Joseph knew it.

Late in April, when the Prophet did finally arrive and a conference was held, Joseph saw the Prophet carry the day. The Saints met in the open air on the ground that had been consecrated for the building of a temple. Before the day was over Joseph felt the members singing with renewed spirit, and when Joseph Smith extended the right hand of fellowship to Bishop Partridge there were tears not only in the eyes of the bishop, but in the eyes of most of the congregation as well. Joseph did not know exactly what had happened, but when Joseph Smith called the Saints to repentance and then praised them for their great accomplishments, the boy sensed that all were reconciled to their prophet. When a vote was called for, making Joseph Smith the president of the high priests in the Church, every hand went up. Later, after the meeting, Joseph heard his father say that the difficulty between Sidney Rigdon and Bishop Partridge had been settled. He wondered how this could be possible, how these men of God could have misunderstandings, whatever they were. Adults were simply incomprehensible to Joseph. How could they admonish the children so sternly and then act like children themselves?

But later, returning home in the wagon, Joseph heard his father repenting, telling his wife that he had been filled with the wrong spirit and that he had had no right to question the Prophet. Joseph felt vindicated, but he was still disappointed in his father. It was hard to get accustomed to the idea that adults could be so much less than they seemed to be.

The next day Joseph Smith came to visit his beloved friends in the Colesville Branch. He was greeted as warmly as he had been the summer before, and his good humor and excitement had its usual effect on everyone. He stayed with Newel Knight's family, but he sat up outside the cabin until late, talking about the growth of the Church and all that was soon to come about. Hundreds more were coming to Zion that summer, he told them. In a few years they would outnumber the other settlers.

The Saints had all heard the story of how the Prophet and Sidney Rigdon, just a month before, had been pulled from their beds in Kirtland, beaten, and tarred and feathered. But Brother Joseph told the story laughingly. One of his front teeth had been broken when the mob had tried to force the contents of a bottle into his mouth. He was certain that it had been some kind of poison. The broken tooth caused a whistling sound when he spoke. Joseph noticed the difference immediately. The Prophet told how it had taken all night to clean the tar from his body and how he had delivered a sermon the next morning with several of the mobbers in the audience. "I know they expected me to abuse them, but I preached repentance and love and peace, and they went away ashamed." Young Joseph was certain that they had.

Joseph Smith rejoiced at Newel and Sally Knight's baby, born the previous October. Sally's other children had died at birth, but Brother Joseph had blessed her on his visit the previous summer, placing his hands upon her head and promising her that she would bear a healthy child this time. And it had happened. Sally had named the boy Samuel because, she said, she had asked for him of the Lord. Joseph Smith was thrilled to see the fine big boy, to see how strong he was. He bounced little Samuel on his knee and laughed as the baby smiled.

And so the evening passed away, with all the news being shared. Joseph Smith told of some great leaders who had joined the Church and would help in the establishment of Zion. A man named Brigham Young and another named Heber Kimball had already begun to serve as missionaries, and the Prophet said they would both be great leaders someday. As he spoke, young Joseph felt confident again that his father's fears and all the talk of troubles were unfounded. Brother Joseph even said that he would be coming to live in Jackson County in time, "when the time is right, when the Lord wills it." Joseph hoped that the time would be soon.

As the group was about to separate, and some had risen to go, Joseph Smith turned to young Joseph and shook his hand. "Joseph," he said, "have you been studying diligently and working hard?"

Joseph could not answer that he had, and he felt terribly embarrassed. His eyes dropped away from the Prophet's intense gaze.

"What's this? Do I see guilt upon your face?" Joseph Smith said, playfully, and then he said more loudly, so all could hear, "I want you to all watch this young namesake of mine as he grows up. I told him last year that he will someday serve a great mission. I know it is true. He has been chosen by God. Don't let him slack off and miss his chance." The Prophet said this in a jovial tone of voice, with a big smile on his face, and yet Joseph knew that it would not be forgotten, that it *was* meant seriously.

Joseph was humiliated. Now everyone knew. He had held out the hope that the Prophet would forget the whole matter, that he would gradually see that Joseph was just not the boy to be called. "May I speak with you alone?" he whispered to Joseph Smith, who had rested his hand on the boy's shoulder as he turned to shake hands with others who were about to leave. The Prophet nodded, as he said good-bye to Jared Carter and some others who wanted to shake his hand before they went home. Then he turned to Joseph, and the two stepped a few strides into the darkness away from the campfire.

"Brother Joseph, I have thought about what you told me last year and I have decided that . . ."

"Joseph, I am afraid it is not for you to decide. Nor is it for me to decide."

Joseph nodded as the Prophet studied the boy's face. "But I am not strong. I can't do it."

"You will be strong, Joseph. I promise you. God will help you. I tell you that because I know it. The next time I see you I want to see your growth; I want you to show that you can be strong."

"I'll try," Joseph said, and he thought that perhaps he could do better, but at the same time he felt a burden, a lump of terrible seriousness. He would try, but he still didn't like the idea.

Chapter 8

One hot afternoon in July Ollie suddenly showed up. Joseph and Matthew met him at the spring, and the three of them returned to the cave they had explored the year before. Joseph and Matthew had gone into the cave several times that summer—it was always cool and made an ideal hideout. They used a bear-grease light, a sort of homemade candle.

Joseph was overjoyed to see Ollie. Matthew had so little fun in him that Joseph had often wished to see Ollie again. Ollie, however, was strangely silent as they made their way to the big cavern where they had found the pool. Joseph chatted, telling Ollie about their winter and spring, but Ollie barely responded. When they reached the cavern Ollie sat down, as he had the year before. He found some little pebbles on the floor of the cave and began to throw them one at a time into the pool, the plopping sound echoing and little rings spreading out on the dimly lighted water.

"Where have you been so long, Ollie?" Joseph asked.

"Working."

"Why don't you ever come over to the swimming hole any more?"

"Pa don't want me to." Ollie seemed different. He was taller, and he had a new shirt exactly like the old one, only less worn, but he seemed older to Joseph. It was partly something in his voice, which was huskier, and partly in a certain aloofness and a lack of interest in the cave.

"Why not, Ollie? Does he need you in the fields?"

"Yeah," Ollie said, but Joseph sensed that this was not the whole answer.

"Is something wrong?"

Ollie threw a rock in the pool, waited to hear the sound echo up above, and then threw another. "I come to tell you something. I come over here three or four times before, but you was always working and so I didn't say nothing and you never seen me. But anyhow I ain't coming no more, 'cause my pa would kill me if he knowed where I was. But I wanna tell you something, just one thing. Tell your pa and ma and all the other Mormons they better find some other place to go and live."

"Why?" Joseph asked.

"You just better do it if you don't wanna get yourselves kilt."

"Killed?"

"Who wants to kill us?" Matthew asked.

"Lots of folks—'most everybody."

Joseph was shocked. He felt his chest tighten—and yet he could not believe it. "How do you know, Ollie?"

"I heard folks talking. Pa says so too."

"Does your pa want to kill us too?"

Ollie threw another rock in the pool. "Yeah," he said.

"Even your pa would kill us?" Joseph said, incredulously.

"I don't know for sure, Joseph," Ollie answered. "He says somebody's gotta run you out and shoot you if you won't go, but he never exactly said he was going to be the one to do it."

Somehow all this wasn't registering very clearly with Joseph. He had heard talk of bad feelings, but it never occurred to him that anyone could hate the Mormons that much. They had never hurt anyone; how could anyone possibly want to hurt them?

"That's unfair," Matthew said. "We have a right to live here as much as anyone." Plop—another stone landed in the water. "Well, is it, Ollie?"

"I don't know. I just come to tell you."

"Because we're friends, right, Ollie? You like us, don't you?" Joseph wanted to know.

62

"I don't know. Not very much. You think you're bet-ter'n me, and better'n everybody else."

Matthew said, "We do not, Ollie. That's stupid. You just hate us because we go to school and because we don't wear buckskins and old ragged clothes."

"See what I mean?" Ollie said, to Joseph, not to Mat-thew. And then he threw a whole handful of little rocks into the pool, making a popping sound like grease sizzling. "Anyway," he said after a few moments, "I told you. You better leave or you're all gonna git kilt, and there ain't no two ways about it. And far as that goes, I don't care a lick about what happens to *you*, Matthew."

"Sure you do, Ollie," Joseph said, "or you wouldn't have bothered to tell us." Ollie didn't answer. They all got up and started back to the mouth of the cave. Joseph was trying to think whether all this that Ollie had said could possibly be true. He doubted it. Ollie knew about trees and Indians and things like that, but Joseph doubted that he knew much about this kind of thing. Maybe his pa had been talking big, and maybe others were doing the same, but it was quite another matter to actually pull the trigger. When they reached the mouth of the cave Joseph said, "Ollie, I think just a few of the old settlers don't like us, but we never have done anything to anyone. I'm sure they wouldn't really try to hurt us."

"Joseph, you're crazy. You better listen to me. They al-ready threw rocks and knocked them new glass windows out of them places up on the Blue—Mormon houses—and told the folks living there that if they didn't get out mighty fast they was gonna get a lot worse the next time. Didn't you even know about that?"

Joseph was astounded. He had never heard the adults breathe a word of such a thing. But Ollie seemed to know. "But why, Ollie? Why did they do it?"

" 'Cause they was Mormons."

"But Ollie . . ."

" 'Cause you're coming in and trying to take over the country—hundreds of you moving in and buying up all the land. And 'cause you want to let the slaves all go, and 'cause you think you're better'n everybody, and 'cause you go around talking crazy about seeing angels and all that kind of truck. And some says you been stealing things—hogs and cows and tools and—"

"That's a lie and you know it, Ollie," Matthew said, almost shouting.

Ollie grabbed Matthew by the shirt with one hand and clenched the other, but he was not convincing. He never really seemed to intend to hit Matthew. "There you go again," he said. "I ought to break your head."

"Don't, Ollie," Joseph said. "You know Matthew's right. You know we don't steal."

Ollie let go. "I don't know if you do or don't, but I know that you ain't got no right to come in and take over the way you're doing."

"God chose Jackson County for us. We can't help that," Matthew said.

Ollie shook his head slowly. His hair hung almost over his eyes, but Joseph could see a tightness, a sternness, something even close to sadness in his steady gaze. "There you are, right there, Matthew. It's talk like that what's gonna get you run out or kilt." Ollie looked at Matthew for several seconds and then he nodded and walked away.

"Hey, Ollie," Joseph said. "Come over next Saturday and let's look for more caves to explore."

Ollie stopped and turned around. "You just don't understand, do you, Joseph." He strode away.

Matthew and Joseph went home and found their father, who was hoeing weeds in the garden behind the house. Joseph ran directly to him. "Father," he said, "have you heard about any of the Saints up on the Big Blue getting hurt or having their houses torn up?"

Brother Williams took off his hat and wiped his sleeve along his forehead. "Yes," he finally said.

"Why didn't you tell us?"

"Well, Joseph, I didn't want to worry you. I don't think it is likely to happen again."

64

"Why not?"

Brother Williams glanced at Matthew, who was standing behind Joseph. Joseph sensed that he was not as relaxed as he was trying to pretend to be. "It was just some old settlers who got all liquored up. Things like that happen sometimes."

"But they said they would come back and do more if we don't leave the county. They said they were going to kill us."

"Who told you that?"

"Ollie."

"I think it would be better if you stay away from his kind, son."

"What?"

"You heard me. I said you should stay away from him. He's not our kind. His father is as godless as any man I know. He's a heathen if I ever saw one. A boy like you—one chosen of God—has no business associating with him."

"But Joseph Smith told us to be friendly with the old settlers and that was how Christians were supposed to be. You even told us yourself that we should—"

"Of course, Joseph. And some of them will be converted. But we don't have to go out looking for Satan."

"But I remember you told us when we first came here that Ollie's pa was friendly to us."

"It turns out I was wrong about that, Joseph. Oliver Markley is about as full of Satan as a man can be, and I suspect that his son isn't much different."

"That's not true. Is it, Matthew?" Joseph turned halfway around but Matthew wouldn't look at him, and he didn't answer. "Well, it isn't. He's our friend." Matthew stared at the ground.

"Joseph, Joseph," Brother Williams said. He took off his broad-brimmed felt hat again and wiped the sweat from his neck with his hand. "When are you ever going to sense your calling? You have been doing a bit better lately, but you still have a spark of rebellion within you. You must master it, son. You must learn to take the advice of those who love you, those who know best."

There it was all over again: the same old accusation. But something in it was worse this time. Always before he had felt that maybe Father was right, that he probably did need to change. But this time his father was wrong, wrong in a serious way. There was something close to hatred in Father's voice when he spoke of the old settlers. And not only that; he had no right to judge Ollie. He didn't even know him. Joseph felt confused—angry, and at the same time scared. Always before, his father had been the force that guided him away from, well, something. It was all not clear in his mind what this change was. And he was still terribly frightened by the prospect of the old settlers attacking again.

"Father," Joseph said, "Ollie said that we will either have to leave or be killed. That isn't right, is it?"

"Of course not, Joseph. This will all pass away. I doubt that anything else will happen. Don't worry about it, son."

"But Ollie says that we're trying to take over."

"Son, we are doing what God has called us to do."

"He says it's talk like that that will get us killed."

Brother Williams took a good look at Joseph. Finally he shook his head and then slowly replaced his hat, pushed it down on his head, and went back to work. Joseph started to repent—he wasn't sure of what. But he wanted to believe he was wrong. He wanted to believe his father was right.

As months went by, however, Joseph knew that things were not as they should be. One night in the fall Newel Knight's haystack was burned. Joseph awakened to the sound of horses and shouting men. He could make out very little of what was shouted, except that he kept hearing the words "Mormons" and "clear out." Then as the horses thudded directly past the Williams's cabin, he heard someone shout, "This ain't the last you'll hear from us." It sounded like fifty, even a hundred horses, but Joseph later heard that there were only about twenty-five or thirty. Brother Williams went to help, but he made the boys stay

66

in their beds in the loft. When he came back he said that
the brethren had simply let the hay burn, there being nothing else to do.

"What are we going to do, Matthew?" Joseph heard
Mother say to Father, whispering, but her voice taut.

"There's more hay," he said.

"That's not what I mean. You know what I mean."

Father didn't answer. In a few minutes he climbed the
ladder and poked his head and shoulders up into the loft,
near the boys' beds. "Settle down now, boys. It's all over.
There's nothing to be afraid of now."

Joseph did not believe that for a moment. He lay
awake wondering what might happen next. They wouldn't
tear down the house, would they? This terrified him. The
house meant so much to him. It had taken a long time to
get it. He liked to sit by the fire in the evenings, when the
wind was blowing outside, and feel warm and safe. He always remembered those terrible days in the shelter when
the Saints had first arrived in the settlement. He never
wanted to be forced out into the open again.

Another concern, although he refused to dwell on it,
was that these men, if they got angry enough, might hurt
him or his family. Sometimes he tried to think what it
would be like to lose one of the family. He would think of
them one at a time and try to imagine the change, but then
he would have to stop because the thought was too painful.
Sometimes he dreamed of a terrifying mob, confused and
numerous, grabbing him and thrusting him deeper into the
confusion, and then he would not be able to find his family
and would search for them amid the hundreds of angry
men; and sometimes he would finally be left all alone, and
he would yell for his father. Once he had yelled out loud,
waking his entire family. His father had had to come up
the ladder to settle him down, and when Joseph had
realized where he was he grabbed Brother Williams with
both arms and cried, his head against his father's chest.

There were other problems, too. The branch was astir
once again with talk of complaining members and some

who were pulling out because of what they thought was unfairness. Brother Gilbert was having difficulties keeping his store running because the Saints often couldn't pay their bills, and it was rumored that he was upset with the Prophet for writing that he should continue to extend credit anyway. The old talk that Joseph Smith ought to be in Zion had begun again, and some said that Sidney Rigdon was having too much voice in how things were done in the Church. Parley P. Pratt had begun a school for elders, but disputes had broken out about how Zion was to be led, and about who should preside in the different branches. The Colesville Branch was relatively free of problems, but word came daily about various members in the other branches threatening to leave. And some did.

To Joseph all this was unsettling. He had assumed that Joseph Smith had straightened out all the problems when he had been in Zion the previous spring. He hated to hear the Saints begin to accuse the Prophet all over again. He loved him and he knew they did too—how could they sound so bitter when they spoke of his staying in Ohio? Once he heard that even Bishop Partridge had criticized the Prophet.

But Joseph Smith did not come to Zion, and more troubles arose. Haystacks were burned and rocks thrown. One night at the Independence settlement riders came with long poles and thrust them through the windows of the Saints' houses, knocking furniture about, even knocking people down. At the Big Blue settlement one night several of the brethren were beaten severely.

As winter began things quieted down somewhat. Good crops had been gathered—in that sense the Jackson County Saints were prospering—but an uneasy tension was evident throughout the season. Joseph wondered with the Saints what the spring would bring.

Chapter 9

The winter passed slowly for Joseph. He pushed himself to study harder than he had in other years, but he could not really say he enjoyed it more. Brother Pratt had returned that fall after being gone for the summer and part of the spring serving another mission. He brought his wife, Thankful, with him and came back to the Colesville Saints and to the school. He was pleased with Joseph and often praised him. The only problem was that the slightest misbehavior on Joseph's part brought the inevitable comment: "Joseph, you have a special calling—you of all people should know better." Joseph had become so accustomed to this that he expected it, but he never liked it, always chafed when he heard it. And he sensed that some of the boys tired of hearing about Joseph's "great calling," although they never mentioned that they did.

That winter Joseph seemed to grow a foot taller. His breeches were suddenly up around his ankles and his sleeves above his wrists. He was even a shade taller than Matthew now, although he weighed much less. Father had managed to buy an old used loom after the harvest had come in. Bishop Partridge had said it was justified, since the Williamses had another child on the way, and so they were allowed to buy it with the understanding that other women in the settlement would also be given the use of it. It was not right for one to have more than others, but a loom was needed and eventually everyone would have one. So Sister Williams spun wool and cotton that winter and wove wool and jean fabric. Then she made new clothes for all the family. Joseph turned eleven in February and he got a nice new Sunday suit for a birthday present. He really wanted a buckskin outfit, but he never would have dared to mention it.

In March an important council was held and seven high priests were chosen to lead the Jackson County Saints. A good many problems were talked out and most of the members felt that the early problems with bickering and disagreeing were over. The only worry now was that the Saints wanted to come to Zion too fast. If too many came this summer it could be very bad. The old settlers would perhaps cause trouble whether more Saints came or not, but new people coming in great numbers would surely cause difficulties. Joseph Smith told the members to wait until permission was granted before moving to Jackson County, but this advice was not always followed.

One afternoon in April Newel Knight rode up on his horse and stopped near a fence Brother Williams was repairing. Matthew and Joseph had been helping, carrying rails, and they were glad to see Brother Knight, glad for the break in their work. "Brother Williams, I don't want to alarm you, but you should be aware that we could have some problems tonight. Some of the old settlers in Independence have called a meeting to discuss what they call the 'Mormon problem.' I think there are some levelheaded people involved, so maybe we have nothing to fear, but some of the drunks and big talkers have been bragging about what they intend to do to us—burn us out, murder us, all kinds of wild threats. As I say, I doubt it's anything more than talk, but I thought you ought to know."

"If they come, what do we do, Brother Knight? Do we shoot back if they start shooting?"

Brother Knight glanced at Matthew and Joseph, who were staring at him, their very bodies stiffened. "Well, I don't know. Somehow I just don't think it will ever have to come to that." He shifted in his saddle and looked down and patted the neck of his horse. He seemed lost in thought for a moment. "I would say that we don't shoot. We don't have much ammunition, for one thing. And it—well—I just can't see us doing that." He glanced back at the boys.

"Now boys, I wouldn't have brought this up in front of you if I hadn't thought you were old enough. You're both getting to be fairly well grown and I think you can be brave with the rest of us. I feel certain we will all get through this thing together. Let's all pray tonight to be delivered from these gentiles. I think we'll be fine if we do."

But Joseph sensed that Brother Knight was searching for words, that he lacked confidence, and this scared Joseph more than if he had said nothing.

Brother Williams said, "If there is trouble, it's more likely to start in Independence or up on the Big Blue. Should any of us be ready to ride up there?"

"I think not, Matthew. It would only be seen as an invitation to trouble from their side. They would say we were raising an army. I just feel that even these people won't hurt harmless people who make no attempt to cause trouble, and who go on living peacefully. I suspect that when we start shooting back, we won't last long."

Brother Williams agreed and Newel Knight rode away. And then to Joseph's amazement his father went back to work on the fence. Joseph felt numb all over. Maybe this would be it; maybe they would come riding in tonight the way they so often did in his dreams, screaming and burning and shooting. He could be frightened by a prairie fire or a tornado or a blizzard, but this was something more: a force that could think and hate and choose to inflict pain. The winter before, Matthew had brought down his first buck. As it lay there in the snow, its tongue hanging out and blood pumping from its shoulder, Joseph had wanted to cry or vomit or run back home, anything to escape just watching those round eyes, staring, glazed. Afterwards he had often thought that there were people who wanted to hunt him down the same way. He wanted to go to them, find the people who hated him and confront them and say to them, "This must be some misunderstanding. We don't want to hurt you, so why should you want to hurt us?"

Brother Williams worked on the fence, replacing sagging and broken rails. "Look at the calf, how it's growing," he said. "Your mother is going to have her milk cow yet. We're going to need more milk soon, with another child coming." Joseph knew his mother was expecting, knew the way he knew that a mare was going to foal, but neither of his parents had ever mentioned it before. It seemed a strange time to bring it up now.

"Listen, sons, I want you to know something I haven't told you before. Your mother gets upset rather easily. When she does, she sometimes gets sick from it. A couple of times before, when she was carrying a baby, she became ill and ended up losing the child. Now, we don't want to make her nervous tonight. I'm afraid we'll have to tell her what we just heard—she'll hear from someone else if not from us—but let's not upset her any more than we must. Please don't make this matter appear to be all that important, and especially do not let on that you are frightened at all. You both must control your own fears. Can you do that?"

They said they could, but Joseph was not sure. He had never been treated so much like a grown-up before, being told something that even his mother could not be told completely, and he had never heard of his mother having miscarriages, and he had never had to act brave for his mother's sake. She had always given him strength. He was not sure that he was ready to be giving strength to anyone else, not as frightened as he felt himself.

Brother Williams warned his wife at supper, telling her much of what Brother Knight had said, though not very frankly or thoroughly. He made everything seem like nothing at all, but Joseph watched his mother grow rigid, her voice becoming tense. She ate little. Brother Williams stayed close to the cabin after the meal and did not ask the boys to do any other chores.

Matthew and Joseph talked about the danger, Joseph admitting his fear, and Matthew reassuring Joseph the way his father would. They walked out back by the garden and sat down in their favorite place by a thicket of redbuds. They were talking when they heard a hiss. They

72

looked back into the woods and saw Ollie leaning out from behind one of the giant post oaks. He motioned for them to come to him.

"Have you heard what's happening?" Ollie said, as they approached.

Joseph thought that Ollie appeared to have turned into a man during the winter. He had hair growing on his upper lip and he was bigger, not just taller, but heavier than ever in his neck and shoulders. "We heard that there will be a meeting in Independence tonight and that there might be trouble," Joseph said.

"Meeting? Hang it, Joseph, don't you folks ever catch on? There's gonna be burning and maybe even killing. Pa says inside a week you'll all be cleared out."

"Is your pa one of them?"

"Kind of, I guess. He says he ain't for shooting nobody 'less he's got to. But he says you just gotta go and that's all."

"But why, Ollie?"

"Joseph, there ain't no use talking about it no more. I told you a thousand times already."

"But nothing I ever understood. We aren't setting any slaves loose and we never stole anything, or anything else you ever told us." Joseph's voice was shaky. His sense of indignation, combined with fear, was almost overwhelming. "Ollie, tell your pa that we're not bad people. Tell him not to burn our house down." His voice cracked so he stopped.

"Joseph, you just don't understand. He only says there's too many of you and you just keep coming, and you're trying too almighty hard to take everying over. You're trying to take from them that was here first, and that ain't right either, Joseph."

"We're not doing that, are we, Matthew?"

"Father says there's room for everyone," Matthew said. "And someday, if there isn't, we can buy the old settlers out."

"But we ain't selling and ain't moving, Matthew, and you got no right to come in and try to take over."

73

"We can't help it. It's God's will."

Matthew and Ollie stared at each other, and Joseph saw the animosity in Ollie's face, even in Matthew's. "Sure. That's what you always say. But pa says Reverend Pixley and some of the others says that's a pack of lies and that people who says such things should be taught a lesson for telling lies about God."

"They're not lies, Ollie." Matthew's jaw became set and his fists doubled at his sides.

"No wonder people want your kind out of here," Ollie said, spitting on the ground at Matthew's feet. He turned and looked at Joseph. "Anyhow, this is the last time I'm coming to warn you. Get out. Tell your pa and your other folks to move somewheres else before this place is running with blood. Some of you is gonna die for sure if you don't listen."

"How come you told us, Ollie?" Joseph said.

Ollie looked blankly at Joseph, shook his head, and tried to say something but stammered. Finally he said, "Just do it, you hear?"

"We can't. Father says we don't have to and that we can't leave."

"Then I hate to see what's coming," Ollie said. He took a long look at Joseph, and then he turned and walked away.

"Thanks, Ollie," Joseph said, but Ollie didn't look back.

As night fell, Joseph's mother became increasingly nervous. She sat in her rocking chair by the fire, mending one of Ruth's dresses. Ruth was watching and continually questioning her mother about what she was doing. Sister Williams answered absently, her mind obviously preoccupied. Her eyes jerked occasionally, as though she were concentrating on every sound she heard. Matthew and Joseph were working on lessons assigned by their father. Since school was out much of the year, he always had the boys read something and do some arithmetic each night, "so as not to let them fall behind."

Brother Williams also sat near the fire, reading the Bible—pretending to read, Joseph thought. His eyes seemed focused on a place on the floor beyond the pages of the Bible.

Joseph worked his problems, but he couldn't read. When the wind blew and moved the trees outside, he found himself wondering what the sound was. Ruth had begun to play with a little rag doll and was prattling to it. When she would move, the puncheon floor would creak and Joseph would suddenly start. Once a log in the fire popped and hissed and Sister Williams jumped to her feet.

"Oh, Matthew, I'm sorry," she said. "This is dreadful." Her voice sounded more angry than scared, and reflected the way Joseph felt. Mixed with his fear was a sense of indignation, a sense that everything that was happening was wrong, unfair.

The long evening disappeared, slowly, but surely. The Williamses finally went to bed, later than usual. They lay awake, listening to each other breathe. Joseph somehow knew that no one was asleep except Ruth. At least an hour went by, and every gust of wind, every movement by one of the other family members, would suddenly startle him into wakefulness. He tried not to think, not to hear; he tried to pray. But it was hardly a prayer—not like the one Father had said before they had gone to bed; it was just a repetition: "Please don't let them come. Please don't let them hurt us. Please."

But Joseph did sleep eventually, and in the morning barn swallows were darting back and forth outside and a cardinal was sitting in the top of a nearby sycamore, warbling for all it was worth. It was warm for April, a mellow sort of day. Newel Knight came by early to say that a rider from Independence had brought the report that the meeting of old settlers had broken up into a "regular old Missouri row." There had been a good deal of drinking, and when the men began to argue about what was to be done with the Mormons, it wasn't long before they were fighting, breaking up the furniture and busting out each other's teeth. Brother Knight enjoyed telling it; Joseph could see that. The Williamses all enjoyed hearing it too, and for the first time in many hours Joseph felt his muscles begin to loosen, his chest begin to gather in breath more easily. "It's an answer to our prayers," Newel Knight said. "I just knew that we wouldn't have to fight them. The Lord has saved us again."

Everyone seemed to agree, but Joseph couldn't help wondering whether this would be the end. Would there be other meetings? Would the old settlers give up that easily?

Chapter 10

The days that followed were full of apprehension, but as no new rumors circulated and no new meetings were called by the old settlers, the Saints began to relax. It seemed that the Lord had come to the assistance of the Mormons; perhaps the hearts of the enemy were finally being softened. Newel Knight told the Colesville Saints as they met in their log schoolhouse one Sunday early in July that he felt the repentance of the Jackson County Saints seemed to be what God had wanted. Letters had been received from Joseph Smith commending the leaders for their renewed spirit and for the letters they had sent asking for forgiveness. He had sent a plat designing the cities that would someday be built in Zion: ten-acre towns with lots for homes one-half an acre each, farms surrounding the towns, and a great temple with twenty-four buildings, a central place from which the work of the Lord would go forth to the world. Joseph listened attentively to it all. He loved to hear about Zion as it would someday be when it was strong and secure.

But Joseph Smith had also sent a stern warning. Everyone must repent and accept the law of consecration fully. Everyone would inherit land in Zion, but the surplus must come back to the Church to be used to help the poor and the new arrivals. Those who continued to hold out and who refused to live this principle were to be cut off from the Church. God's work would go on without them.

The letter also said that two new bishops had been called to help Bishop Partridge lead the Saints. Isaac Morley and John Corrill were the two new ones, but the exciting news for those in the Colesville settlement was that

Newel Knight and Hezekiah Peck were both to serve as counselors, each to one of the new bishops. It was a fine honor and all were proud of their brethren. Never, to Joseph, had the dream of Zion seemed so real, so possible. Twelve hundred Mormons were now in the county, farms were thriving, homes were being enlarged and improved, a newspaper—the *Evening and Morning Star*—had begun publication, and the organization and operation of church affairs were finally smoothing out.

Brother Knight closed the meeting by admonishing the members to be pure and godly, to avoid all evil and all contention, to strive to live in harmony with each other, that the Lord might bless them to prosper and withstand the enemies who would foil the work of God. He told them to take to heart the advice received from the Lord by Joseph Smith in a new revelation that year. It advised the Saints to avoid tobacco and strong drink and to make their bodies tabernacles of the spirit. If they would live in righteousness and purity, the old settlers could not prevail against them.

Joseph left the meeting greatly encouraged. He felt happier than he had in months, happier than ever, it seemed. He thought it was a good sign that he had enjoyed a sermon. Perhaps he was beginning to grow up; perhaps he was becoming the kind of boy God wanted him to be.

But then, before the week was even out, rumors were circulating again. A "secret constitution" was being passed about by the old settlers, denouncing the Mormons for all the old complaints. Signers agreed to take any means to drive the Mormons from the boundaries of Jackson County. All signers were to meet on the twentieth of July in Independence, where a plan would be drafted to finally rid the county of Mormons, "peaceably if possible, forcibly if necessary."

Word also began to spread among the Saints that the Reverend Pixley had published letters in eastern newspapers describing the Mormons as degenerate blasphemers and wild fanatics, a danger to all decent Christians. And

78

the Reverend Finis Ewing had published a tract that he was taking from house to house in the county. It concluded: "The Mormons are common enemies of mankind and ought to be destroyed." Every minister in the area had taken up the cause and was preaching to the congregations that such perversions—belief in modern-day prophets, healings, speaking in tongues—could not be tolerated by right-thinking Christians.

But the one issue that stirred the people most was slavery. In the July issue of the *Evening and Morning Star* William Phelps had published an editorial admonishing the Saints to "avoid all appearance of evil" when it came to the issue of welcoming "free people of color" to Jackson County. He had meant that the Mormons were being accused of trying to free slaves in the county and that they should simply stay out of the whole question. But the old settlers interpreted his statement as a stand against slavery, and the word spread quickly among the many settlers who could not read that the Mormons were calling for the freedom of the slaves in the county. Even a special edition of the newspaper on July 16, forcefully denying that this had been meant, made no difference to those who wanted to believe what they had first heard.

As July 20 approached no one talked of anything else. Mormons prayed for another miracle, while the old settlers vowed in public that this would be the end of the troubles once and for all because the Mormons would no longer be tolerated. They would leave or they would die.

Joseph continued to hope that somehow this all could be headed off. For some time a plan had been forming in his mind. It was really a daydream more than a plan. He had always felt that the old settlers would change their minds if they could only get to know the Saints and come to understand that they were good people, undeserving of such terrible treatment. It seemed so obvious to him that there was room under the same stars for everyone, that there was simply no need for all the hatred. In fact, it was so obvious to him that he could not imagine the troubles

79

continuing if the old settlers could ever come to see the matter clearly. In his daydream he saw himself standing before their meeting, speaking to the multitude of angry settlers. He simply told them in a straightforward little speech that all the people, Mormons and old settlers, could live together in peace. He told them what fine men Bishop Partridge and Newel Knight were, and he told them about his father and how he always taught his sons never to hurt anyone. "We are not bad people. We do not want to take anything from you. We can all be friends." He had given the talk many times in his mind, each time a little differently, but the basic words were always about the same. It always seemed so convincing in his own mind that he began to believe that it might actually work. No one could hear his words and still want to kill him.

Of course, he knew that he couldn't do it—they wouldn't let him and he wouldn't dare—but he thought it over more and more as the day of the meeting approached. His fear was growing, and with it began to grow a sense of desperation. Someone ought to do it. He told Matthew someone ought to try it, but Matthew said that if it were the right thing to do Bishop Partridge would do it—he surely knew best. Joseph accepted that for a day or two, but then he began to wonder whether God had not planted this idea in his heart because he was the one to do it. Hadn't Joseph Smith told him that he was called of God to serve a great mission? How did he know this was not it?

Joseph prayed more seriously than he had ever prayed before, asking over and over whether or not he should do it. He began to feel he had his answer, that he should, that it was his mission to be a David going forth to save his people. But at times he wondered. How did you know for sure when you had an answer from God?

He probably would have dropped the whole idea had it not been for his fear and for the feeling that if he did not try, he would never know whether he had missed his chance to serve the Saints. He kept telling himself that maybe a boy of eleven, speaking honestly and meekly, would have more power to persuade these settlers than a fully grown man would. He compared himself to Joseph Smith, who had been called by God at a very young age and had not hesitated in serving as he was called. Sometimes he imagined what the Saints would say about him, how they would honor him if he were the one to turn the tide and save them from the gentiles' wrath. Then he would feel ashamed, knowing that he should not think of the honor, but only of saving his people.

Just when he had decided that it was a silly idea and that he would stop thinking about it, word came that a braggart in town had said that every Mormon house would be burned to the ground within hours after the meeting. Above all Joseph feared the loss of his house. He never again wanted to be turned out into the open, to live in tents and shelters, not to have a real home. Who—what decent person—could deny him just that little wish? And so as evening fell on the nineteenth of July Joseph was beginning to think maybe he would go to the meeting.

His plan was simple and still a little vague. He would watch for a chance to get away the next morning, walk the twelve miles to town, and be there by one o'clock when the meeting was to be held. He would then walk to the front, identify himself, and ask to speak to the group. If they denied him the chance to speak, at least he would know within himself that he had tried to do what he could. He decided that his Father in heaven would have to work out the details as he had for Nephi in the Book of Mormon.

Things began well the next morning when Father sent Joseph out to hoe weeds in the garden but took Matthew along to cut hay. He often did this, but it was a special relief to Joseph today because he had feared he might end up under his father's eye all day. Mother might notice that he was gone, but she would probably just think Father had sent him to do some other chores. He would not be missed until noon, and by then he should be in Independence. He had taken a sheet of paper with him that morning, and before he slipped away he wrote a note and left it on a stake at the far end of the garden: "I had to go and do the work of the Lord today. Do not worry. I will come home tonight. Joseph." He did not want them to become alarmed and begin searching for him, nor did he want them to know exactly where he would be.

Joseph began the long walk along the old oxen trail into town just a few minutes after his father disappeared from sight with Matthew. And his good fortune continued—a man in a wagon came along and gave him a ride. At first he was hesitant, afraid the man might be going in to the meeting, but the man said hardly a word, seemed not to be interested in knowing anything about the boy.

Before eleven o'clock Joseph was in Independence. All was going well, and to Joseph this was a sign that God was helping him and that he was doing the right thing. He tried not to think what he would say to the old settlers: first, because it made him nervous to think about it, and second, because he wanted the Lord to put the right words in his mouth. What he did try to think about was how happy all the Saints would be when they heard that the old settlers had decided not to drive the Mormons from the county. He imagined the Prophet when next they met, folding Joseph in his arms and saying that he had always known the boy would fulfill his mission. Joseph's confidence was growing even though his stomach was fluttering.

Already there were many people in town. Joseph walked past the stores on the town square and saw that the taverns were full and men were even standing in the street waiting to get in. The meeting was to be held by the courthouse, and by noon people were already gathering amid the tree stumps on the courthouse square. Some of the men had formed a circle and Joseph could see from a distance that two men, their shirts off, were fistfighting. The crowd roared and cheered them on as they pummeled each other, kicking up dust. There were even women in the crowd, some of them seemingly enjoying the fight as much as anyone, but most of the women stayed back and gathered in little groups to talk.

Joseph heard so many ugly remarks about the Mormons that his courage gradually began to fade, but the one image he was to remember long after was that of a big man with long red-brown hair and a wide, full beard. "I tell you what," he said to three or four men standing in sort of a circle in front of Lucas's store. "I'm ready to do what's gotta be done. They're getting out and mighty fast, and that's all there is to it. I ain't for killing 'less that's the only way—but if it is, then I'll wade in blood up to my neck!" The other men nodded their agreement and swore to do the same. Joseph walked by. He wondered what people would do should they recognize him, but in his homespun clothes and with his feet bare he blended in fairly well with the community.

Chapter 11

By one o'clock Independence was overflowing with people. Wagons were parked far down the hill away from the town square in all directions, and horses were hitched or hobbled everywhere. At the square were hundreds of people, mostly men. Joseph was later told there were four or five hundred, but all he knew at the time was that he had never seen so many people in one place in his life. His resolve was completely gone by now; he could feel his heart pounding in his chest, in his head. Somehow God was going to have to take over and finish the rest of the job. Joseph just wanted to run home, run from Jackson County, back to New York or to Kirtland, where the Prophet was, or to any place where the people didn't hate him.

A man stood up on a big wooden box that had been placed in front of the courthouse, and shouted for all to be quiet. Joseph was at the back of the crowd, standing on a stump, stretching to see. He didn't know the man, but later others called him Mr. Simpson. He wore a suit and a top hat, and he spoke better than the trappers and farmers and mule skinners did. Joseph saw Mr. Lucas from the store—Colonel Lucas, they called him—and he had heard Mr. Flournoy's name and Lilburn Boggs' name before. Both had sold property to the Church. There were at least ten others in suits standing in the front. He had seen some of them in the stores before, but he didn't know their names.

Many in the crowd had been drinking, and they were not easy to quiet down, but finally Mr. Simpson called the meeting to order. "We are here today to deal with a serious matter, one that is of concern to all of us. We intend to act fairly and with reason, but we all realize that the time for firm action has come."

84

"Time for burning some houses down," a huge voice bellowed from the crowd and a cheer went up.

"Now let's not have any more of that," Simpson shouted, and the crowd quieted again.

Joseph didn't know how he would get to the front, but he knew he would have to do something soon before the men got themselves any more worked up. He kept saying to himself that he had to start, but his body kept standing there, as though it were refusing the command of his brain. His legs wouldn't move. It had never been like this in his mind. He had imagined a rather orderly meeting, like a Mormon conference, and he had pictured himself walking down an aisle to the front.

Then suddenly he was moving and he wondered if God had made the decision, because he felt that he himself hadn't. Simpson was suggesting that a resolution needed to be drawn up and a vote taken. There were shouts that the resolution ought to simply say "get out or else," but Simpson persisted. He began to suggest names of possible committee members to write up the resolution. Joseph slipped between two men, jogged to the left, slipped between two more, and then was engulfed in the heavy, stinking air of big men all around him. He struggled a little way further ahead, but before he could get clear he heard Simpson say, "All in favor, say 'Aye.'" A shout went up and then Simpson said, "We adjourn then until the resolution is written up. It shouldn't take long. Stay nearby." The crowd began to flow back against Joseph and he tried desperately to thrust himself forward, but it was too late. A man caught him and said, "Hey there, where're you going to?"

Joseph gave up and moved back away from the courthouse. He knew what he had to do now. As soon as the crowd thinned out a little he walked all the way to the front, to one side of the speaker's stand. He pulled his flannel hat down low over his face, worried that someone might recognize him, but no one seemed to pay any attention. He breathed a little easier but his heart had never

85

stopped pounding, and in the rising afternoon heat he felt weakness coming over him. He had not eaten since early that morning, but he did not think of that. In fact, he did not think of anything any more. He just wanted the people to come back; he wanted his chance. He hoped something would come out of his mouth, but he refused to try to practice what he would say. It simply scared him too much to imagine the situation, especially knowing that he no longer had the words in mind.

Eventually a stir brought Joseph's eyes up, away from the dust at his feet, and he saw men in suits coming across the square. He felt the crowd move in around him as he turned toward the box. There were a few other boys around and the men seemed not to care. No one said anything to him, but he kept his head down.

The men in their long-tailed suits stood behind the box and talked for a minute or two, and then Simpson stepped back up on the box and faced the crowd. It was Joseph's time. "Mr. Simpson, could I . . ." His words only barely choked from his throat, and they were drowned as Simpson shouted the men to order. As they quieted Joseph tried again. "Mr. Simpson, I would like to . . ." He stopped again. Simpson was shouting, not hearing Joseph. "Mr. Simpson," Joseph shouted, his tight voice sounding high-pitched, surprising even himself. Simpson looked down, puzzled.

Then a man stepped from behind the speaker's box and took Joseph by the arm. "What is it, son?"

"If I may, sir, I would . . ." His voice stopped working again. He swallowed. "I would like to say something . . . to everybody."

The man stared at him. Joseph took a deep breath and waited. "You're a Mormon, aren't you?"

"Yes," Joseph said, "If I could only . . ." But the man was moving through the crowd, pulling Joseph through by the arm, the men in the crowd stepping aside but brushing against Joseph. The man pulled Joseph until they were fifty feet or so away from the crowd before he stopped. Joseph felt everything as if through a haze. The man had him by both shoulders now, staring in his face.

"What in the world do you want here, boy? Who sent you?"

"No one, sir." Joseph fought the tears but felt them on his face, saw through them vaguely. "We're not bad people, sir. Please don't burn our houses. Please don't hurt us."

The man was short and slight. He had long sideburns, grayer than his hair. His teeth were stained and crooked, but his eyes were gentle, light brown, under bushy yellow-gray eyebrows. He stared softly into Joseph's face.

"Son, go home. You can't understand what is happening here. We don't aim to hurt anyone."

"But sir . . ."

"Go home. Go home," he said softly, patting Joseph's shoulder. "When you move to a new place you will be happier." He walked back to the crowd and pushed his way to the front. Joseph sat down on a stump and let himself cry. He was humiliated and disappointed, but he was not leaving yet. He had given up, but he was not sure that God had. He would just wait and see whether there had been anything at all to the inspiration he thought he had received.

But for the moment he gave up and let the tears come, sobbing aloud without worrying whether anyone heard him. It was a relief to cry; it would have been more of a relief to cry in his mother's arms, and in that sense he wished he were home. But to be home was to face his father and account for his foolishness, and he was not ready for that.

Simpson began to read the resolution and Joseph heard it only distantly. It said that action was taken after cool deliberation, and with recognition that the law would move too slowly to deal with the matter of the Mormons. It said that too many Mormons were coming to Jackson County, that they were low people, poor, and little elevated above the conditions of slaves. Joseph began to listen. He couldn't imagine that they could say such things. The Mormons were corrupting slaves, it said; they were agitating the Indians. They would soon take over the county by sheer force of numbers. And the warning was given. No more Mormons were to come to the county. Those who were there must pledge to leave as soon as they could arrange to do so. The *Evening and Morning Star* must cease operation. The last part was hard to understand, something about those who speak in tongues, but the idea seemed to Joseph to be that the Mormons would have to get out or face the anger of the old settlers.

The resolution was passed with a deep-voiced, rumbling "aye," and then twelve men were named to form a committee to visit the Mormon leaders immediately and get their reply. Most of the men in suits, Lucas and Owens and the other store owners, soon headed toward the Mormon settlement west of town, a sizeable part of the crowd following. The rest spread out, many heading for the taverns; very few were leaving town. Joseph heard one man say, "This ain't the way to do it. We need to just get started." Joseph wondered exactly what that meant.

Joseph continued to sit on the stump for most of the afternoon. He hated to leave until he was certain that his chance was really lost. It was a terribly long, hot, numb sort of afternoon. He watched the men loiter in the town square. Someone got up a horse race and a good deal of money was bet, but the race was held east of town and Joseph only heard people talk of it. He also heard that a cockfight was taking place in one of the taverns. He watched all this without thinking. He just sat in the dust and heat and waited, not even worried any more that someone might recognize him.

It was late in the afternoon when the leaders returned. The crowd gathered more slowly, but eventually it was almost as big as it had been before. And it was more out of hand. Many more were drunk now, and the yelling and cursing was almost out of control. The men had grown impatient waiting all day, and they screamed for some real

88

action. Joseph heard one man say, "I didn't come up here all day to watch all these highfalutin store owners talk. I come to get started moving them Mormons out, and that's just what I still think we ought to do."

Simpson tried to get the crowd calmed enough so that he could talk to them, but time and again someone shouted out a vow or curse and the others cheered and joined in with their own curses. "Let's get started. Let's burn 'em out," was the most common thing Joseph heard them shouting. Finally they listened, but only briefly; and when Simpson said, "They claim they need time to make a decision and say they want to talk to Joe Smith," there was a cry of outrage. "They wanted . . . listen to me . . . they wanted three months time to answer us . . . now listen . . . but we told them they could have a quarter of an hour . . . will you keep it quiet long enough for me to tell you what happened . . . so anyway, when they came back they said they could not give us an answer that they would leave. Now we need to decide how exactly we want to handle this . . ."

But he was drowned out by the bellowing crowd. Someone yelled, "Let's go shut down the press," and others took up the cry. Suddenly the crowd began moving toward the southwest corner of the square where the press was. Those in front began to run, and in a moment the whole crowd was jogging, dust rising with the screams—terrible, high-pitched screams, sounds that Joseph had never heard come from men. He stood up on the tree stump he had been sitting on and watched them mob in around the press. The businessmen who had directed the meeting followed the mob but watched from a distance. They made no attempt to stop anything. Joseph saw Sister Phelps appear at the door and watched her being escorted through the crowd. He ran then and tried to get to her, but she was moved toward the west and Joseph lost sight of her. She was carrying a baby, Joseph thought. Where was Brother Phelps? Would they hurt him, or had they already?

Two men ran up the stairs on the outside of the building and used a bar to pry open the door. Joseph was just behind the mob now and he could hear the men shout, "Bust 'er open, John." The door gave way and the mob cheered and at least twenty more men ran up the stairs. In a few minutes several men appeared carrying the press. They lugged it down the stairs and dropped it in the street, where others began to beat on it and kick it. Everything was carried out. The type was scattered in the street and paper was thrown in all directions. Joseph found out later that some of it was the first edition of the Book of Commandments, the first publication of Joseph Smith's revelations. A few copies were saved by some of the members who sneaked up later to gather them from the street.

Then Joseph saw a man on the roof who began to wave his right arm in the air, much to the mob's delight. He was yelling something that Joseph couldn't hear, but in a moment he heard someone say, "He said if this was the wrong thing to do he wanted God to smite his arm and make him stop." The men bellowed their laughter. Then they yelled for him to get on with it. He began ripping up shingles with his bare hands. In minutes others had joined him, some with tools or boards taken from inside the press room, and the roof was ripped away in no time, leaving the rafters bare. Men swarmed over the building like ants and began slamming at the brick walls with anything they could pick up. A big log was carried to the front of the building and thrust through the front window; then it was used to ram against the back wall. Bricks began to fly and the mob below surged back. Within half an hour the entire building was rubble; it was unimaginable to Joseph. He had never seen men work with such passionate force; he had never imagined that men could look so wild, hate so openly. He was sick inside, weak and sick. How could he have thought to stop this? This was a force beyond all reason, beyond any power. It seemed that not even God could stop it. It appeared that the power of darkness he had always heard of had really risen and taken over.

Then there were shouts that Gilbert's store should be

next, and the mob moved northward, somewhat less frantically than before. The store was broken open and the goods were carried out. Bolts of fabric were rolled open in the dirty street and dry goods were scattered in all directions. Joseph saw men leaving with some tools they apparently decided they wanted. Then to Joseph's surprise someone shouted, "That's enough here. He promised to be out in three days." The crowd yelped with joy and surged away to the south again, for the moment just following each other with no sense of direction. Shouts were soon heard that they should go get some of the Mormon leaders and that they should tear down the blacksmith shop that was nearer the Mormon settlement. They picked up their pace then, surging back toward the corner where the press had been ripped apart and then veering to the west where the Mormon settlement and the blacksmith shop were.

Joseph had stayed behind the mob, and now as they reversed their direction he moved back to the corner where they had made their turn. He saw a man in a suit standing near the rubble that had been the press. As the mob came by him, the man waved and yelled to them, smiling, "Now I guess they know what our Jackson boys can do!"

"That's right, Mr. Boggs," someone shouted back. "They know we ain't just talking now."

Joseph was terrified. Seeing men ripping down buildings filled him with disgust and amazement. But now they would be after some of the Church leaders. Joseph wondered what that meant. He followed at a distance, watching the dust rise up around the mob, hearing their shouts fade as he let them move away. It was a mile to the Partridges' home, and Joseph knew they would head directly there.

By the time Joseph came up behind the mob again, they had already pulled Bishop Partridge from his house and some of them were moving back toward town. Another brother, a man Joseph hardly knew, named Charles Allen, was also being held by the arms on both sides and was being marched alongside Bishop Partridge.

Some of the mob broke off toward the west, where other Mormons lived, but Joseph moved back toward town, staying ahead of the big group that had Bishop Partridge. One of the men holding the bishop's arms was wearing a suit. Joseph hated to think that even these men could take such active part with the town ruffians. He watched Bishop Partridge carefully, but he saw no emotion, no sign of either fear or anger. He was tall, taller than most of the men there, and he walked as quickly as the mob around him, as though he were leading them. By contrast, Charles Allen seemed frightened, his head continually turning to one side and then the other, as though he expected someone to attack him from behind.

When they reached the town square everyone stopped by the tree stumps near the courthouse. Nothing happened; the men just stood, somewhat more quietly, expectantly. Joseph wondered if they were waiting for someone or for something to happen. And then it occurred to him: maybe they were waiting for someone to bring a rope. Suddenly he was running. He had to do something now. He ran for the speaker's box, which was still sitting near the courthouse. Maybe he would have his say yet. He dove onto the box, landed on his stomach, and clambered up to his feet.

"Listen," he began to shout, but almost at the same moment a cheer went up from the mob. Joseph saw two men coming across the street, one carrying a bucket and the other carrying something white that Joseph could not identify for a moment. Then he realized that it was a pillow. The mob was going to tar and feather the two brethren. In a way this was a relief—at least they would not be killed. Joseph gave up again; he was not all that far from the crowd of men, but they were not looking his way and, of course, they would not listen. He finally admitted what he had known all day: they would never have listened to him. He was a powerless boy, eleven years old, trying to head off a power immensely bigger than himself. He was foolish to have ever thought otherwise. His sense of impotence, of smallness, was painful; it left him numb. He stood atop the box and watched.

Chapter 12

"Paint 'em up good, Shepherd," men were shouting.
The man they called Shepherd and another man, apparently named Connors, moved through the crowd until
they faced Bishop Partridge and Allen. Russell Hicks, as
they called the man in the suit, said loudly enough for all
to hear, "You have two choices. Either renounce your
Mormon Bible or leave the county." A rough sort of grunt
of affirmation went up from the mob; then someone
shouted, "Call on your God now to save you." Several
more took up the same cry and the others laughed, but
Bishop Partridge stood calmly before them, seemingly un-
bothered. Then the bishop began to speak and the crowd
hushed as they strained to hear him.

"I have done nothing to deserve your hatred," he said
confidently. "I have never done harm to any man here. But
I am prepared to suffer for the gospel of Jesus Christ. If you
abuse me, you injure an innocent man." Joseph expected
an outcry of contempt; surprisingly, however, little was
said in response. But the man they called Connors, a
massive man with a bald head and a huge, fat face,
grabbed the bishop's coat from behind, jerked it down, and
tore it from his arms, spinning Partridge around and
knocking him off balance so he slipped to the ground. Connors grabbed him roughly, yanked him back to his feet,
and began to rip his shirt, but suddenly Partridge stepped
forward and turned around. As calmly as before he said,
"Don't leave us naked here in the street. Otherwise, you
may do your will."

To Joseph's amazement Connors simply stood and
looked at Partridge. Then Shepherd, without removing

any more of the bishop's clothing, began to daub tar on the front of his shirt. The same was done to Allen. The crowd was almost silent. The tar was slopped heavily on the heads and faces of the two men, and over their clothes, and the pillow was opened and feathers were strewn upon them, but it was all done rather routinely, with little of the passion that Joseph had observed all afternoon.

When the men were finished, Partridge walked from the crowd with Allen behind him, and the crowd simply opened up and let them walk away. They looked grotesque, like huge molting birds, and yet the bishop, tall and lean and erect, walked before them with a dignity that contrasted so obviously with all that had gone on all day that Joseph felt certain everyone saw it. He saw it. He felt it. He was glad for the first time to have been there.

And that was the end. The mob broke up and soon people were leaving Independence in all directions. Joseph ran after Bishop Partridge and Charles Allen. He caught them at the edge of town, where some of the other members had surrounded them. They had horses, and Bishop Partridge was being helped up on one.

"Bishop Partridge," Joseph yelled, and the little group all turned as the boy ran toward them.

"Joseph Williams, what are you doing here?" someone said.

"I came to . . . to help, if I could."

"Joseph, that was foolish. How could you . . ."

"It's just as well," the bishop said. "Joseph, hurry home and tell your branch what has happened. Tell them to warn the Whitmer settlement. Some of these people may head your way next—if not tonight, perhaps another day." He spoke in his usual voice, but Joseph could see that his face, under the terrifying blackness of the tar and the grotesqueness of the feathers, was contorted with pain.

"Did they hurt you, Bishop?"

"Not much, Joseph, but they must have put something in the tar, lime or acid. It burns dreadfully. We need to start cleaning it off. You hurry."

One man on a horse led the bishop's horse away, and another was taking Charles Allen double on his horse. "Thank you, Bishop," Joseph said. "I am sorry. I am sorry they hurt you." But Bishop Partridge did not hear.

Joseph began to run, and he ran for a long while before he slowed to a walk. He walked as hard as he could, but it was very late when he finally made it back to his home that night.

Needless to say, Brother and Sister Williams were upset when Joseph got home. They were overjoyed to see him at first, and his mother took him in her arms and held him close. But soon the questions began, and Joseph told the story badly, failing to make it totally clear at first why he had gone and what he had seen. His mother kept saying, "Oh, Joseph, how could you? You might have been killed."

It took some time to get the whole story straight; Joseph finally had to start over and tell it all in order. Brother Williams said little, mostly sat quietly and listened, but Joseph could see the muscles in his jaw ripple under the blackness of his beard. He wondered if his father was feeling anger or some other emotion, and wondered whether it were directed at him. Joseph was tired and numb and weak, too exhausted and upset to worry about punishment.

Joseph told about Bishop Partridge facing the mob, and about the warning that the mob might come to the Colesville and Whitmer settlements next, and then he was silent and so was the whole family. Matthew had been sent to bed earlier but had not slept; he had gotten up when his brother had come home. Ruth had been awakened by the noise of Joseph's arrival and was sitting in her mother's lap, half awake.

"Father, I know you think I was foolish," Joseph said. He could see the light from the fire flickering on his father's face, but he could not see any clue in the man's eyes as to what he was thinking. "But I really thought I could help. I thought if I just could make them understand—and well, I thought that Heavenly Father wanted me to go."

96

"Joseph, you cannot talk to these people. They're in Satan's grip and past all reason." There was ice in his father's voice.

"I know," Joseph said, but then he felt a need to correct himself. "Except that's not exactly how it was. Only a few of them seemed to be so . . . so crazy. The rest of them just seemed to let the others make them that way. And some only stood and watched. The man who talked to me was a good man. He was sorry. I know he was."

"Of course some are worse than others, Joseph, but where was the man to stand up and try to stop it? Boggs and Simpson and Lucas and Owens are educated men, should know better. They're no better than the rabble." He had reached down to pick up a log to put on the fire, but suddenly he thrust it at the fire, sending the sparks flying. Joseph saw his father's eyes flaring in the sudden burst of light. For a moment the boy saw a flash, an image of faces he had seen all day. And his reaction was as it had been before: shock, fear, and even disgust.

But almost immediately Brother Williams calmed and he put his hand on Joseph's shoulder. Joseph felt the needed gentleness. He did something he had not done for some time: he grabbed his father around the waist and pushed his head tight against the older man's chest. "Father, I thought God wanted me to do it, but he didn't."

Brother Williams held Joseph for quite some time, then took him by the shoulders and held him back so he could see him. "You don't know that, son. It was right for you to want to help, though of course you couldn't. But perhaps it was good for you to be there, and maybe God even wanted it that way. We never know exactly what he has in mind for us. You saw some terrible things today, but you saw something good as well. An experience like this may be of lasting importance to you."

"But why does it all have to happen? Why doesn't God just stop it?" This was the question that had been building up in Joseph's mind all day, especially during the long walk home. It was the worst question of all.

"I don't know, son." Joseph saw that his father's face was red with the firelight on it, and that his eyes suddenly looked distant. "We can't judge that either."

"But we should, Matthew." It was Joseph's mother, and her voice was strident. "Why did he bring us out here into this wilderness just to see us persecuted and abused?" Everyone was silent. Sister Williams was sitting in her rocking chair holding Ruth, staring ahead at the wall, refusing to look at anyone's eyes. Brother Williams let go of Joseph. "Matthew, I do not want to bring another child into this world in this place. I want to go home."

"I do too," Brother Williams finally said. "That's just what I would like to do. But Elizabeth, the Prophet sent us here to establish Zion. If the gentiles run us out, then I don't know what we do after that. I don't know what God's plans are for us any better than you do—and I can certainly understand Joseph's confusion—but I *do* know what we have to do for now. We have to stay here until the Prophet tells us to leave. If we are killed for the sake of the gospel, we won't be the first to die that way."

Sister Williams said nothing; she didn't disagree, but she didn't agree either. She just continued to stare at the wall, clear-eyed and angry.

Two uneasy days followed. Brother Williams worked in his fields and spoke little to his wife, who answered him in terse sentences, avoiding any real conversation. Joseph felt out of breath, all tight inside as though his insides were brittle and about to splinter. Matthew asked him again about every detail of his day in Independence, and he rehearsed it over, and then Newel Knight had him do it again. But Joseph couldn't feel it very much any more. What he felt more strongly was his mother's smoldering anger. He could run from the mob to his family and home, but he couldn't run away from what he saw happening in his own family.

On the evening of July 23, John Corrill rode into the settlement and stopped at Newel Knight's cabin. In a few minutes all the Colesville Saints had gathered. Brother

Corrill told them that the mobs had formed again and that two companies of men, most of them wearing red or black paint on their faces, had ridden through the Independence settlement threatening to beat the Mormon leaders unless they promised to get out. Reverend Pixley, carrying a red flag, had led one of the groups. They vowed to lash each Mormon leader one hundred times. Edward Partridge, John Whitmer, William Phelps, Sidney Gilbert, and Isaac Morley had offered themselves as ransom, but the offer had been turned down. A meeting had been held and the leaders had been given the alternative of death and destruction for all the Mormons in the county or a commitment to leave. The Mormon leaders had signed the agreement, seeing no other option. All leaders and their families, under the agreement, were to be out of the county by January 1, 1834. No Mormon newcomers were to be allowed into the county. Store owners could sell out their goods, and agents could stay to settle the sale of land, but all other Mormons must be out of the county by April 1834.

The Saints listened in silence. When Brother Corrill finished there was no response at first, just terrible quiet. "After all this work," Hezekiah Peck finally said. He spoke for the rest.

"Well, we're not entirely certain, Brother Peck," Brother Corrill said. "This is mob action, not legal action. They have no right to do this. They can hold a gun to our heads and make us sign an agreement, but that does not make it a legal document. Some of the brethren are going to see Governor Dunklin. Maybe we can get some help. We're being robbed by hoodlums, and the government ought not let it happen. Oliver Cowdery is leaving tomorrow for Ohio to see the Prophet and get his advice."

It was this glimmer of hope that the Saints clung to. Government by mob would surely not prevail in the United States. They knew that Boggs was attorney general in the state and would support the mob's actions to the governor, and they knew that Samuel Lucas, one of the ringleaders, was a county judge; nonetheless, the state and federal governments should rise above such lawlessness. This was the tenuous trust of the Mormons, and so they made no plans to leave.

In the next few weeks the Saints received encouragement from Governor Dunklin. He wrote the Mormon leaders and told them to test the legal system and prove that mob violence could not rule. The Saints wondered whether courts in Jackson County would ever rule for them, but they felt better having the governor's opinion that they were in the right in not leaving the county. Four lawyers from Liberty, Missouri, across the river from Independence, were hired to work for the Saints. It cost one thousand dollars to retain them because the firm felt that their business would be damaged by taking up the cause. But Doniphan and Atchison, the two young lawyers in the firm who would head up the Mormon defense, seemed like trustworthy men, men who could perhaps deal with even the corruption of the frontier court system.

The Saints continued to go about their business as usual, but an uneasiness was always about. Every church meeting, every private discussion among neighbors, every dinnertime chat seemed to eventually turn to the problem. The most persistent argument among the Saints, the one strengthening idea, was that God would help them because he wanted them to stay in the county. Joseph wondered. He had seen what had happened in Independence and no hand had stopped the mob.

By October it was becoming clear to the old settlers that the Mormons were making no plans to go anywhere. Rumors spread that lawyers had been retained. A newspaper, the *Western Monitor,* had taken up the Mormon cause and advised the Saints to stand pat, not to allow themselves to be driven out by the Jackson County rabble. This only inflamed the old settlers all the more.

On Sunday, October 20, Newel Knight spoke to the Colesville members at evening services. The Saints had gathered as usual in the little schoolhouse. "Brothers and sisters, the leaders in Zion have reached a decision. On Monday, October 28, we plan to file suit in circuit court, seeking redress for property damages and a restraining order against those who have attacked the Saints. As of to-day we are announcing publicly that we have no intent to leave the county. It may be that the Jackson County gentiles, or at least the troublemakers, when they see that the law is on our side, will back down. There are some good people here—do not underestimate their power to influence those who ignore the law. Nonetheless, to be realistic, we all know that trouble may lie ahead. We have decided to defend ourselves. We will harm no man first, but if he comes upon us he may expect a fight. May the Lord open a way that this never becomes necessary, but if it does, may angels fight with us, for we fight for what is right."

He paused and looked around the congregation. It was a cool evening, but no fire had been built and most of the Saints were bundled up. Joseph sat next to his father; he looked up at him and saw that his face was resolute, firm as always. Beyond him was his mother, her face cold and enigmatic. Since July she had softened very little, perhaps talking a bit more but still rebelling inwardly. She had never again said that she wanted to leave, but she obviously had not changed her opinion. She went about her work quietly but stiffly. If she had shown her anger openly it would not have been as bad, but Joseph felt a loss of emotion in her that was painful to see. Sometimes he saw his parents walk into the woods, away from the children, his father doing most of the talking, but when they came back his mother seemed unchanged. Joseph knew that it could not be too much longer until the baby came, and he knew that this, more than anything, was on his mother's mind.

Brother Knight continued. "I fear what lies ahead for us. This will be a time of testing, I suspect. The Lord will sift us and find out who is strong. Pray for strength, brothers and sisters, and prepare yourselves."

101

He paused again, letting the words sink in. Joseph felt what everyone seemed to feel: a sense of the ominous. *Are we really strong? Am I strong?* Joseph wondered. In his mind he could see the mob again, the faces, the anger. He felt little strength when he imagined himself facing that.

Then, in a new voice, Brother Knight said, "Brethren, please gather immediately after this service for a short meeting. We must discuss the plans for our defense."

The Saints sang "The Towers of Zion Soon Shall Rise," a new hymn by William Phelps. Hezekiah Peck was called upon to pray. He was usually one for lengthy prayers, but this time he was brief and ended his prayer by saying, "And if some of us must die, Lord, may we rest in peace in thy bosom." Joseph felt chilled clear through. He wanted no part of resting in peace. Above all, he feared that it might be his father who would be called on to fight and to die.

After the meeting, Joseph and Matthew and Ruth walked home with their mother. When their father returned a little later, he asked the boys to come outside. They walked away from the house and stood by the little thicket of redbuds.

Brother Williams faced his sons. "Boys, you have heard enough to scare you today, and I don't want to add any more to that, but I must discuss something with you. Let's assume that nothing bad will happen, but should troubles arise I have decided what I want you to do. The men are setting up a watch and we are also prepared to ride to the other settlements should problems develop there. You are both too young to help, but you are big enough that these mobs may not recognize your age, and they might fire upon you. It puts you in a bad position. You cannot fight, but you could be abused by these madmen. So this is my decision: should any troubles develop here, I want both of you to hide in the woods. If I am gone you may be tempted to defend your mother and Ruth, but not even these men are likely to bother them. They are the best protected by simply staying in the house and by not having you two nearby. I know that sounds cowardly, but I feel certain that it's the safest approach and, in the long run, the bravest."

"I don't want to do that, Father," Matthew said. Joseph looked at Matthew and saw him looking more like Father than ever. He was growing up. He was thirteen now, still not very tall, but his voice was becoming deep and his face was less childish. He had always had an old face for his age, because of his seriousness, but Joseph noticed a confidence about his eyes that he had never noticed before.

"I know you don't, Matthew. I don't blame you. But promise me you will. If I am lost, Matthew, someone must be left to carry on in my place."

Matthew stood stubbornly for a few seconds, but finally he nodded his head in agreement, and Father shook his hand. Joseph shook hands with Father too, but it was not the same, didn't mean the same thing.

Brother Williams bent then and looked directly at Joseph. "Don't try anything on your own again, son. All right?" Joseph said he would not, and he did not plan to, either. He never planned to try to be a hero again.

Chapter 13

All through the following week a nightly watch was set around the Colesville settlement. Brother Knight's grist mill seemed an obvious target for an attack, so at least two men stood watch there each night, Brother Williams taking his turn with the others. All remained quiet, but reports came back from Independence that threats were being made again and that the settlers' anger was rising as it became clear the Saints were not leaving. On Sunday Newel Knight told the Saints that a meeting had been held the day before, that only about fifty old settlers had shown up, but that they had voted to a man to remove the Mormons by whatever means necessary.

The Colesville members were nervous, certainly frightened, but they hoped that the small turnout at the meeting was a good sign. The next day was the day for filing suit, and everyone prayed for the best. Some of the men from the Colesville Branch, including Brother Williams, rode in to Independence to be there the next day, and all day those who remained behind at the settlement wondered what was happening. For Joseph it was one of the longest days of his life. He knew what the mob could do, remembering their faces. He had always wished that his father were different, a little more lighthearted, but now he only wanted him back. Sometimes he tried to imagine what his family would do were his father not to return one of these times, but the thought created such insecurity that the boy had to force it away.

But when Brother Williams returned that night he seemed more relaxed than he had been in some time. He said that a few old settlers had been around, that some terrible oaths and curses had been shouted, but that very little had happened otherwise. The brethren were encouraged, and the speculation was that the less ardent enemies had been frightened away by the legal action. Perhaps they had heard of Governor Dunklin's encouragement to rely upon the courts. Perhaps only the most fanatic were still trying to raise opposition, and maybe they were too few to make any difference.

It all sounded very good to Joseph. He watched his mother, hoping to see some sign of change, but she said nothing, and the cold look that had become so familiar now did not alter. Later, Joseph heard her say quietly to Brother Williams, "I felt some pains today. Please don't leave me any more, Matthew. The time for the baby cannot be too far off." Her voice was not tender nor was it hostile; it was just empty.

"Elizabeth, you know I may have to leave. If I do I'll have someone stay with you. But I cannot help it. If I am called to go help somewhere, I simply cannot turn Brother Knight down. I'm hoping that won't be . . ."

And then Joseph heard his mother's voice stab at his father: "No, Matthew, don't turn anyone down. You couldn't do that. Except for me. It's all right to ignore my wishes."

Father glanced at Joseph, saw that he had been listening, and looked back at his wife without answering, his face firm as a stone.

The watch continued to report each morning that all was calm, and by Thursday everyone was growing confident that the law had triumphed. A number of small incidents had occurred in Independence, but the very fact that they were minor matters seemed to indicate that nothing was being organized.

Joseph was sleeping better, dreaming less. Then in the dark, early Friday morning, suddenly he was startled awake by a pounding on the cabin door. He awoke disoriented, his breath held in, terrified.

"Brother Williams!" he heard a deep voice say.

In a moment Brother Williams was out of bed and at the door. Joseph crawled to the opening and looked down from the loft where he slept. Matthew was beside him. "What is it?" Father asked, as he opened the door.

"The Whitmer settlement has been attacked. Some of the people have come here. Can you take some of them in?"

"Of course, Brother Peck."

By now Sister Williams was out of bed and had pulled a shawl around herself. She stirred the fire and flames climbed up, lighting the cabin enough that Joseph could see a woman step in the door. She was heavy, he thought at first, and then he realized that she was holding a baby and that she had a blanket wrapped around her. A boy younger than Joseph, maybe eight, and two girls, one close to Joseph's age and one about four, all tried to huddle against their mother at once, standing just inside the doorway.

"Come in, come in. Come to the fire," he heard his mother say. For the first time in weeks she sounded like herself.

"Thank you, Sister Williams," the woman said. "I can't tell you how . . . how . . ."

"Don't talk. Come here to the fire."

Brother Williams had gone outside, apparently to talk to Brother Peck. When he stepped back in the little girl who was about four grabbed her mother and let out a tight, harsh scream.

"No dear. It's all right," the mother said. "This is Brother Williams. He is our friend."

Joseph could put most of the story together easily enough. He could imagine what had happened. He had seen it in his own mind many times. The mob had come and driven them all out in the night, just as he always feared they would do. Where was the father?

Soon blankets were brought out and the little children were put down to sleep by the fire. Sister Williams took the baby, and the mother sat in the rocking chair, close to the

106

children, reassuring them until they could settle down. Brother Williams had dressed and gone. "It's all right now," the woman kept saying, but the little girl kept whimpering. Once Joseph heard the little boy say, "They won't come here, will they, Mama?"

Joseph got back into his bed, but he didn't sleep. The little children finally settled down. The mother came back and took her baby, and the two women sat side by side on the bed.

"I know I have seen you at conference," Sister Williams said, "but I don't know your name."

"Parker," the woman said. "John is my husband. He is still at the mill with the other men. My name is Margaret. We just come this summer. From Pennsylvania."

"Was anyone hurt, Sister Parker?"

"Oh, Sister Williams." Her voice strained to a stop for a moment. "They beat Brother Page senseless. I only hope he lives. They come right in the house and ordered us out. They knocked John down and kicked him. We got out and then they started tearing everything up. In no time at all they had the cabin half tore down. They just acted crazy— shouting such awful . . . oh, it was . . ." She began to sob.

Joseph lay awake after that, even after Sister Williams talked Sister Parker into lying down. His hopes were shattered. He only wondered how long it would be until the mob came to his house.

Brother Williams came in before daybreak and Sister Williams sliced bacon and fried it and made corn bread, which she baked over the fire. When the sun came up everything seemed a little less frightening. Even the children seemed more relaxed. Joseph didn't talk to the girls, but he asked the boy what his name was. "Jared Parker," the boy said, but he refused to look at Joseph. After breakfast he walked outside with Joseph, however, and Joseph asked him whether it had been frightening when the mob came. Jared nodded. He was blond, with no eyebrows, it seemed, but he had brown eyes, the color of maple syrup. The eyes seemed flighty to Joseph, like bird's eyes. "Did you see them tear down your house?" He nodded again, quickly and just once.

"What did they say?"

"Get out or we'll kill you."

Joseph got little more out of Jared, but he didn't try
much harder. The men said it was time to get the
governor's help, that the law was the only answer now. A
militia had to be brought in quickly.

By evening word came that Independence had also
been attacked. Mormon houses had been brickbatted,
poles had been thrust through windows, doors had been
broken down, and Gilbert's store had been attacked and
damaged again. Some of the brethren had caught a man
by the name of Richard McCarty in the act of throwing
rocks through the windows of the store. They had arrested
him and taken him before the county justice of the peace,
Samuel Weston, but Weston had refused to issue a warrant
against McCarty. But then, as Brother Williams pointed
out, Weston had been one of the leaders of the mob when
the press had been destroyed. Joseph wondered how the
law was going to help them, if that were the case.

That night Joseph slept fitfully. Brother Williams
stayed up all night, watching with many other men at the
mill. When he came in for breakfast Joseph could see that
something had happened.

"We had a little trouble last night," Father said, and
Joseph could see that he was playing it down as always. "A
couple of the old settlers came on Parley Pratt and hit him
a hard lick over the head with a rifle—cut a terrible gash in
his head. Parley and some of the others were able to
subdue them, though, and we held them overnight and let
them go."

"What do you suppose they were up to?" Brother
Parker asked.

"I couldn't say." Brother Williams glanced at his wife.
"Some think that maybe they were sent ahead to spy and
see how many were armed and waiting, and that if we
hadn't taken them in the act they would have gone back

and brought a whole mob in. I don't know. They might have just been a couple of troublemakers by themselves."

There was silence, everyone apparently recognizing how close they had come to finally being attacked. "But I wouldn't be concerned," Brother Williams continued. "We have sixty men here now and over half of them have some kind of firearms. Brother Pratt and Brother Marsh are riding to Lexington today to see the circuit judge. We should get help soon."

Joseph suspected that his father was not as confident as he wanted everyone to think he was. In any case, Joseph *did* worry. In fact, he did very little else.

Chapter 14

Saturday night was quiet at the Colesville settlement, but by Sunday morning the word went around that the mob had attacked the Saints at the Big Blue and that David Bennett, a Mormon who had been sick in bed, had been beaten and fired upon, the bullet leaving a gash in his head but not penetrating his skull. One house had been partially unroofed before some members from the Whitmer settlement had ridden in to help. Guns had been fired on both sides, and one of the old settlers, who was in the act of ripping a roof from a house, had been shot through the leg. At the same time a number of Mormon leaders had been arrested in Independence for the "false arrest" of Richard McCarty, the man they had caught damaging Sidney Gilbert's store.

Word had reached Independence that the Mormons had risen up and had shot and killed a man. This, of course, was not true, but throughout the county the old settlers were now saying that they must defend themselves against the Mormons. Rumors also spread that the Indians had joined with the Mormons and were set on helping them drive all the old settlers from their homes. The lives of the church leaders in jail seemed in great danger.

As the Saints met in church that Sunday some of the men remained to guard the houses. It was a grim day, with the threat of war facing the Saints. Some talked of getting out before it was too late, but most continued to believe that the law would finally prevail if they could just hold on a bit longer.

On Monday morning Matthew and Joseph did not have to walk to the spring for water. It had been raining all night and the rain barrel was full. The rain subsided for a while, but it was misty and cold outside. The fall leaves were mostly gone now, except for the dark brown ones still clinging to the pin oaks. After breakfast the boys walked out into the gloom and went to the mill, where many of the men gathered each day. It was very difficult for men to think about cultivating the soil or working at their homes at a time like this. Mostly the men speculated about what was to come, whether help would come soon, whether they would be attacked.

The boys listened to the talk for a while, but it only made Joseph more nervous. "Let's go, Matthew," Joseph said.

"Go where?"

"I don't know. Home, I guess. There's nothing to do here."

"I like to hear what the brethren have to say," Matthew said.

"Well, I don't."

"Does it scare you?"

"No."

"Yes, it does."

"Well, you didn't see the mob in Independence, Matthew. You don't know what it can be like. I don't like to think about it."

"That may be fine for you, Joseph—you're only eleven. I'm old enough to fight and I may have to." He said it casually, and Joseph could hear that Matthew was trying to imitate the talk of the men.

"Father told you not to. He said that you should hide in the woods with me. And you promised him."

"I know, Joseph. And I'll keep my promise. But I am not going very far, and if I have to come back and help I will. I wouldn't ever do anything foolish like you did when you went to Independence, but I'm not a coward. I'll be ready if I am needed."

Joseph took the insult in stride. He could accept that, but he did not like Matthew's plan at all. He remembered his father saying that if he were lost someone must carry on.

The day went quickly in spite of the fact that Joseph had little to do. He dreaded the night most and somehow always felt more confident in the day. Matthew and Joseph were back at the mill in the afternoon when a man on horseback was seen coming toward the settlement. There were others behind him.

He began yelling long before he reached the mill, and Joseph recognized that it was David Whitmer. "We need help. There's trouble at our settlement." Horses were saddled quickly, and in a few minutes a little group of about thirty men was ready to ride, Brothers Williams and Parker among them. Brother Whitmer said they had gotten into a skirmish with some old settlers when they had gone to the Big Blue settlement to help again, and that the old settlers had chased them home and were tearing houses down. Their group had been so small that they had been scattered in all directions, and now no one was left to protect their settlement.

Joseph watched the men ride away, his father on a borrowed horse, since he still owned only a mule. Just before he left he had told Matthew, "Go home and tell your mother, but don't alarm her. Remember what I told you. If they should come here, you take Joseph and hide in the woods." Then he had looked at Joseph. "Do what Matthew tells you. I'll be all right, Joseph. Don't worry."

Joseph felt angry. He wanted to yell at his father as he rode away, to tell him that he couldn't promise any such thing. The confusion was unbearable. There seemed no end to the fear and the frustration. When would this all come to some sort of conclusion?

The boys went home and told their mother and the Parkers, and they all waited. The sun was gradually going down, and Joseph dreaded the darkness. He wanted to sit by his mother, close, but he was embarrassed. He watched her revert to her coldness, saying little to Sister Parker, preparing supper mechanically, encouraging the children to eat, eating nothing herself. Alice Ann, the four-year-old Parker girl, wanted to be held and was whining, but Sister Parker was holding the baby, who was crying. The noise made Joseph nervous; he went outside, but just as he stepped out he heard a distant rumble, like the sound of thunder miles away. But the sky had cleared. Then he heard more, sometimes single pops, and he knew it was gunfire. In five minutes it was all over.

He did not go back in. He told no one. He stood by the house and listened. An hour went by and it was dark. There were few birds around now, and the cicadas were gone. Everything was quiet, waiting for winter to open up. Joseph breathed steadily, listened, and waited. Finally he heard horses. Without thinking, simply assuming that it was the brethren returning, he ran to the mill. As the horses approached, suddenly it occurred to him that maybe these were old settlers coming to attack. He stood stiff for a very long few seconds until he finally heard Newel Knight's voice. As they came close he scanned the men, looking for his father, but he could not see him. It was very dark and all was confusion; Joseph felt panic coming over him as he searched in the dark, still not seeing his father. "Father," he called out, "Matthew Williams."

Nothing. And then, "Joseph?"

It was his father's voice and Joseph took a deep breath. His father came out of the dark and hoisted Joseph up in his arms like a little boy. "Joseph, what are you doing here?" Joseph had never heard his father's voice sound so tender. He put his arms around his neck but said nothing. "I told you to stay at home with Matthew," Father said, his voice returning to normal. Joseph squirmed and his father set him down.

"I heard the guns," Joseph said.

Brother Williams nodded. Joseph couldn't see his face very well, but he sensed that his father had understood.

Brother Parker approached and said he would take care of the horses if Brother Williams wanted to go back to let the women know they were home. Brother Williams agreed, and he and Joseph walked through the settlement to their home.

"Father," Joseph said, "did anyone get hurt?"

"Yes, Joseph. Brother Barber and Philo Dibble were both shot. I doubt that either will live. Brother Cleveland and some others were wounded, but they should be all right." Brother Williams hesitated and then said, "And we shot two of them. I think they are both dead."

"Oh, Father, no," Joseph said. He stopped and Brother Williams turned to him. "Now they will get us for sure."

"We had no choice, son. They were beating people, ripping houses apart, and then they fired upon us and we fired back. Only half of us even had guns, but what could we do? We had to fire back to chase them off."

"But you know what you told me. If we ever fight them we will lose. You said that to me. I didn't think we would ever start killing *them.*"

"I don't like it either, son. Unless we get help soon, I suppose we *will* lose. As I saw what was happening all I could say to myself was that now we had gone too far. But I don't know what the alternative is, Joseph. We are dealing with devils. If God wants us here, he—"

"I don't think he does, Father. Why won't he help us?"

"Oh, Joseph, I don't know. You always want to know what I can't answer. You and your mother. I have to do what seems right, but I can't find all the answers for the two of you. I keep saying to myself that there must be some good reason for all this—I suppose to test us—that's what Brother Knight says—but I don't know."

"We need Joseph Smith here."

"Yes, in some ways that might help. But it wouldn't really change anything."

Joseph pondered that briefly, then said, "Let's leave. Let's go back to New York or Ohio or somewhere else. We could leave in the morning."

"Joseph, we are called of God to be *here.* I have told your mother that and now I tell *you* once again. We cannot just back out on that. If our leaders decide we must leave, we will go where they tell us to, but we are part of God's work, and we don't just go out on our own and break away. Some are doing it, but we will not. I would like to as much as you, but we simply cannot."

"Called of God," Joseph thought to himself. Being called of God was the biggest problem a person could be forced to live with, as far as he was concerned.

The next day, Tuesday, a rider came from the Big Blue settlement. Rumors were abroad that the Church leaders, who had been jailed, were to be executed. The men from all the branches were going to attempt to free them. When Brother Williams rode away, Joseph felt a deep sense of foreboding. He felt that he would never see his father again.

Chapter 15

All day Matthew and Joseph sat at the edge of the woods watching out across the prairie for their father. It was cold but sunny and a light breeze made the prairie grass, which was yellow now, move in waves. Jared Parker spent some time with Joseph and Matthew, but he got cold and went in. They went in to eat lunch, then came back and watched all afternoon, talking little. Over and over Joseph saw an image in his mind: There would be a battle near the courthouse and his father would fall in the muddy street. A bullet would strike him and he would slowly slump into the mud. Joseph tried not to see it, but over and over it repeated itself in his mind. He wondered how long it would be before they heard what had happened. The other fear was that evening would fall and they still wouldn't hear anything.

Finally, late in the afternoon, Joseph and Matthew spotted horses in the far distance; the boys stood and watched, hoping, without saying anything to each other, that it was the Colesville brethren and not the mob. Soon they could see that Brother Knight was leading the way; then they saw their father's black beard and his floppy black hat. They glanced at each other and nodded, too full to say anything.

As their father broke from the others and headed toward them, they could see concern in his face. He dismounted at the house as the boys ran to him, but he said nothing to them, simply strode inside.

"Elizabeth," he said, "we have no choice now. We will have to leave the county. We must get all in order tonight and leave in the morning. We will have to pack what we can in the wagon and leave everything else."

Sister Williams stood staring at him, emotionless, it seemed. Brother Parker had returned the horses to their owners. He came in looking solemn, his eyes fixed. "Mary," he said, "let's head for the Whitmer settlement now. Christian Whitmer says we can stay the night with him and leave with our people in the morning."

"What has happened?" Sister Parker asked.

"Lucas and Pitcher led a so-called militia today. It was really just the mob that has been making the trouble, dressed up in uniforms. They stopped us outside Independence. Lyman Wight was leading our people and he met with them. They told him that if we would turn over our guns they would disarm the old settlers and enforce a peace. They promised—Boggs and Owens and all of them—swore that there would be no more killing, but the condition was that we leave the county right now. They have our leaders and they have us outnumbered by a wide margin. We only had about forty guns for a hundred of us. We just didn't have a choice."

"Before we could even leave," Brother Williams said, "they were riding through the Independence settlement, shooting and threatening. All the members have taken up camp at the temple lot, trying to protect each other. That militia will never take away any guns from their own people. We have to get out now. Maybe we can get help— maybe from the governor—and maybe we can come back soon, but right now if we don't clear out they will start shooting to kill."

That night the Williamses were up very late, discarding most of what they owned, storing items in the house but assuming that they would never see them again. They carried their few valuables to the wagon. Sister Williams had left most of her cherished things back East long ago, sold to raise money for the move. But she had kept one set of nice dishes, and these she packed carefully in a little wooden box she had used to bring them from Ohio and New York.

Joseph was relieved in a way; the trouble would be over

and they would all get out alive. But where would they go? Where would they sleep the next night?

They got up early the next morning, ate breakfast, and packed a few last items. Joseph knew that his mother was suffering. Her time had to be near. Yet her face revealed nothing. Brother Williams hitched up the mule to the wagon and tied the calf to the back. It was a cold morning, dark and cloudy and threatening rain. Joseph was standing near the wagon, taking a last look at the cabin, when he heard horses. He saw men in buckskins riding across the prairie, heading toward the mill. "Father," Joseph said, but Brother Williams was already watching them.

"Matthew, Joseph, get back into the woods. I will call you when it is safe. Hide yourselves well."

A gun was fired and then two more. "They're just shooting in the air. Don't worry. Now get going." Matthew and Joseph ran toward the woods, but Matthew stopped at the woodpile and grabbed an ax that his father had not yet loaded on the wagon. He then hid close to the back of the garden, just barely into the woods, crouching in a place where he could peek out. "Get behind me, Joseph. And stay down."

They could hear men shouting down by the mill and occasionally another gun was fired. Joseph breathed in jerks, listened, wondered whether they were shooting in the air now. Gradually the sound was closer, and then he could hear the voices nearby, cursing and yelling.

"Clear outta there—*now!*" And another barked, "Get amoving right now."

"We are leaving," he heard his father say, loud and firm. "We are packed and ready. We will be out of the county by sundown if we can."

"You don't need no wagon. Just get agoing."

"What kind of men are you?" Brother Williams said. "We are leaving with next to nothing, leaving most everything we own behind. We gave up our weapons and you promised to give up yours but you didn't. What is it you want? Are you men or animals?"

118

Then Joseph heard a heavy thud and a grunt, and suddenly Matthew was up and running. Joseph leaped up, unclear as to what was happening, but he saw Matthew running directly toward several men on horses, all of them facing away. He had the ax in his hand. He swung it at a man on horseback, striking him in the back with the blunt end. The man tumbled over the horse's neck to the ground. The horses jumped and danced in confusion, and one bolted ahead. Matthew swung again wildly, missing a man's arm and rifle, but he brought the ax back and struck the rifle and knocked it away. Joseph jumped out of the underbrush where he had hidden and ran toward the horses. He found a rock and threw it hard, hitting a horse in the back leg. The horse leaped, slipped in the mud, then reared up and snorted as the rider cussed. A gun fired and Joseph came up from finding another rock; he spotted Matthew still on his feet, still swinging the ax. The horses were dancing crazily, sometimes dangerously close to Brother Williams, who was on the ground. Joseph saw blood on his father's head and face. Joseph threw another rock and then ran closer, not knowing what to do. Another gun sounded and Matthew dropped. Joseph screamed and a man spun and fired at him, a bullet whizzing by him.

Joseph couldn't move. He stared at the man, whose horse was jumping frantically, a big man—Ollie's pa, Joseph realized vaguely—trying to control his horse, not able to shoot again. And then Matthew was up and running toward Joseph. "Make them chase us," he cried, and he and Joseph ran towards the woods. A bullet sounded in the leaves just over Joseph's head and he ran hard, as fast as Matthew. He knew they were heading for the cave.

They were soon well along the trail. They could hear horses thumping in the woods behind them, but Joseph knew he and Matthew could make it to the cave because the horses would be slowed by some parts of the trail where limbs hung low.

In five minutes they were in the comforting and yet frightening darkness of the cave, feeling their way along

119

the sides. They got to the cavern and the pool, then sat down. "Will they come in?" Joseph asked, his breath still coming hard.

Matthew didn't answer for a time, and then he said, "Maybe. I'm bleeding. Maybe they can follow the trail. Probably I'm not bleeding that much. Maybe they won't find the cave." He stopped to breathe. "They can track us in the mud and leaves maybe, if they want to. But it's dark in here and they don't have lanterns."

"Where are you bleeding, Matthew?"

"In the leg. At the top."

Joseph could see nothing. "How bad is it?"

"I don't know. It doesn't hurt all that much yet. It must have missed the bone because I ran all right. I think it went through the inside part of my leg. It feels like it's bleeding plenty."

"Will they go back and kill Father?"

"I don't know, Joseph. Maybe he . . . I don't know."

"What did they do to him?"

"Hit him over the head with the barrel of a rifle."

"Did you kill that man you hit?"

"No. I saw him get up."

And then they could hear voices, muffled at first, but soon echoing from the mouth of the cave. "They musta went in here. I sure hate to let 'em get away. Fred's hurt bad."

"Let's get a lantern or something and take a look back in here. I'll go fetch some kind of light from one of them Mormon places."

"All right. Go ahead."

"What can we do, Matthew?" Joseph said.

"I don't know. Maybe we can make a run for it."

But they both knew that it wouldn't work, that they would never make it. Then Joseph remembered. "Matthew, you can get through that little opening back there. I told Ollie a lie that day."

Suddenly they were both feeling their way to the back of the pool, and Matthew found the opening. He got down

120

on his hands and knees in the cold water, grunted with pain, but squeezed his way through, just barely able to keep his face out of the water. Joseph followed him. In a few feet a new cavern opened up. The boys felt with their hands until they found a dry place to sit down.

"Are you all right, Matthew?"

"It hurts more now. I need to get the bleeding stopped somehow." Joseph felt him move and knew that he was taking his coat off. "If I tie these sleeves tight around it, maybe it won't bleed so much."

Joseph didn't know whether that would work. He knew they had to get out of the cave as soon as possible and get help.

"Matthew, is Father dead?"

"I don't know. I don't think so."

"If they find us, will they kill us?"

"They can't in here. They're too big."

They waited. Before long they could hear the men in the cave.

"I don' wanna go much further back in here. It's getting too low to walk."

"Wait. Here's blood."

"Well, all right. Now be careful. Let's go on, but watch. They prob'ly got a rock or something and prob'ly waiting back here somewheres to try and jump us."

They grunted and scraped along until they came to the first cavern. "They ain't here."

"They gotta be somewhere here. Look at that blood."

"But there ain't nowheres else to go 'less it's back there through that little opening."

Joseph heard them slosh through the pool, heard a man grunt as he apparently bent to look. "That's it, for sure. But we ain't getting through there."

Silence. And then, "Well, you two little cursed brats, you stay back there and bleed to death or starve to death, but some of us is going to wait out at the mouth of this cave for a week if we have to. And by the way, we just went back and fixed up your pa some more."

Laughter echoed for a few seconds, and then they sloshed back out of the pool and left the cave.

"What can we do, Matthew?"

"Let's wait a little while. They won't wait around very long. They just want to scare us."

Joseph didn't know what to expect; he thought about praying and then he gritted his teeth and said to himself, "What good would that do?"

The boys let half an hour go by. They could no longer hear voices. They decided to try moving out to see if the men were really waiting. Matthew had to get help soon.

As Matthew stood he groaned. And as he bent in the cold water, Joseph heard him gasp for breath. "Joseph, I don't think I can crawl now. It hurts too bad."

"Try, Matthew. You have to."

Joseph heard Matthew move in the water and then he let out a little moan. He tried again, taking heavy breaths, the air catching in his throat. And then his voice cracked as he groaned, "My leg won't bend that far, Joseph. I can't do it."

"Do it on your stomach. Pull with your hands. I'll try to help from behind."

Then they heard a voice in the cave and they both fell silent.

"Joseph, Matthew. Where are you? It's Ollie."

Joseph looked up quickly. "Don't say anything," Matthew whispered, apparently thinking what Joseph feared. Maybe Ollie had been sent in by his pa to get them to come out.

"Joseph, Matthew. Where are you?" He must not have a light, Joseph decided. "Are you in here, tell me? Pa said you went back in a little opening. Where is it?"

He wouldn't say that, Joseph thought, if he were against them. "We're in here, Ollie," Joseph yelled.

"Joseph," Matthew said, "what are you doing?"

"You can get out now," Ollie called back. "I told Pa I'd watch the cave. Come on, you can get away."

"How do we know that, Ollie?" Matthew asked. "How

do we know you're not helping your pa get us out?"

There was a long silence, and then Ollie said, slowly, "You never do change, do you, Matthew. You just stay in there, if that's what you think. I didn't have to come back here to help you. I'm gonna catch it for this."

Joseph heard him walking through the pool. "Wait," Matthew said. "My leg is hurt. Can you help pull me out?"

Matthew began to pull himself in the water, breathing hard and making headway, and then his legs slid away and Joseph knew that Ollie had pulled him through. Joseph followed.

In a moment they were all standing in the darkness. "How bad you hurt, Matthew?"

"I'm shot in the leg. It's bleeding. I tied my coat around it but it's still bleeding, I'm pretty sure."

"Let's get out to the light and then I'll see what I can do."

The boys followed Ollie through the dark. Joseph could hear Matthew's breath coming strained from deep inside him as he walked. When they got close enough to the mouth of the cave to have some light, Ollie took off his coat. He had on a red flannel shirt, a new one. He unbuttoned it and took it off and then got Matthew to lower his breeches. Matthew's long underwear was soaked with blood all the way down his leg. It was difficult to tell what the wound was like.

Ollie wrapped his shirt around Matthew's leg and then tied the sleeves tight around it. Matthew had to hold onto his brother; as Ollie pulled the sleeves tight Matthew gripped Joseph tighter and moaned. But Ollie helped him get his breeches up and helped him walk. "Your mule is still down by your house," Ollie said. "You better unhitch it and head out of here."

"Did you see our father?" Matthew asked.

"No."

"Mother?"

"No one was down there. I tried to git here to tell you Pa and them others was coming, but I come too late. When

123

I come I seen your wagon all ready and your calf and all, but no one was around. Then Pa come up from the woods and wanted to know what I was doing. I told him I just wanted to see what was happening, and that's when he told me about you being in the cave and I should watch. He said they'd be back, and if you tried to get out to stop you."

"How soon will they be back?" Joseph asked.

"I don't know, but you better get going."

When they got back to the wagon, Ollie helped Matthew lean against it and then he started unhitching the mule. "I know it's going to be hard to ride, Matthew, but you'll make lots better time than if you try to pull that wagon all full of gear. I just don't know what Pa might do if they catch up with you."

"Where can we go?" Joseph wanted to know.

"Father must be alive, and they must have forced them to leave without the wagon."

"Or Brother Knight took care of his body," Joseph said.

"I don't think they could have had time for that. Father was planning to head for the mouth of the Big Blue and then across the Missouri into Clay County. We'll head there and find them."

"Thanks, Ollie," Joseph said.

"Ollie, I'm sorry," Matthew began, too embarrassed to look Ollie in the eye.

"Just hurry," Ollie said. He had the mule unhitched. But then horses were audible again. Ollie tried to get Matthew up quickly. Spreading his leg was agony for Matthew, but he got astride the mule, and Joseph was clambering up behind him when Ollie's pa and the three other riders came into sight. For a moment they thought of trying to make a run for it, but they knew it was too late.

Matthew looked at Ollie, who was standing with his black coat wrapped around him, open at the neck, his bare skin showing. "I'll do what I can," he said.

"What's going on, Ollie?" his pa yelled, as he reined up his horse. "You helping these two?"

124

"Let 'em go, Pa. They's just . . ."

He took a blow across the face from his pa. Ollie stepped back. "Don't you know these two clubbed Fred Brandt with a ax? We just took him home. He's all crippled up. Like to broke his back with a ax. Don't talk to me about what these two is." Markley took his rifle from the long holster that hung on one side of the saddle. "I think we had enough of these two."

Ollie stepped to the side of the mule, next to Joseph and Matthew. "Pa, don't shoot 'em. It ain't right."

"I'm more of a mind to shoot you right now, Ollie. You head home, get your gear, and clear out. I don't hope to see you again."

"All right, that's fine with me. But don't shoot Matthew and Joseph. They was just trying to help their own pa."

Markley spat on the ground, rubbed his hands over his stubbled chin. "I weren't planning on shooting 'em. If you don't shut your mouth though, I might. Get going now. You never have knowed who was buttering your bread. You never could see what these Mormons is trying to do. It's them or us, Ollie. You never could see that. Now git."

Ollie glanced at Matthew and Joseph, and then he walked away.

"What we going to do with these boys, Markley?" one of the men wanted to know.

"Well, I'd say that long as we's going to Independence we ought to just take 'em along. Show 'em there's laws here. Show 'em you can't hit a man with a ax and not end up in jail."

And so it was decided. Markley led the mule and rode the twelve miles to Independence. Before they got there, Matthew was passing out at times and Joseph was clinging to him, holding him on the mule, pleading with the men for help.

"He'll get a doctor soon as we get there. Best thing now is just get him there. Now quit your bawling or I'll throw you down a well like I done your pa."

The other three men laughed. "Where is my father?" Joseph demanded.

"I told you. I throwed him down a well. He's dead, boy. You ain't never going to see him again." The men laughed again.

Joseph hoped that this was an indication that his father was alive. Surely they wouldn't be able to joke about it if they really had killed him. Not even these men could do that. And yet Joseph wasn't sure, and his sense of indignation was overwhelming. "What's wrong with you?" he screamed at Ollie's pa. "How can you be so mean?"

"Listen, boy," Markley said, twisting in his saddle to look at Joseph. "You just shut your mouth. I didn't mind you folks when you first come in here. I just thought you was loony. I didn't know you was going to try to take away my land. I'm just defending what's mine, that's all. Too many of you come and you tried to take everything. You talk about being mean? Who was it killed Hugh Brazeale and Tom Linville up there by the Big Blue?"

He believes it, Joseph thought. *He really believes he is right.* Everything in the world seemed upside down. But as he held Matthew he hoped that they could at least live, that Matthew and his father would be all right, that they could all get back together somehow. He wondered about his mother, and little Ruth, and the baby. And finally Joseph prayed, silently. He told God he was sorry for his faithlessness and asked that they all might live.

126

Chapter 16

Markley had been talking about taking the boys to jail, but when they reached Independence he took them to a house instead. It turned out the house belonged to a man known as Doc Noland, but to Joseph the big surprise was to find that the doctor was the same man who had told him to go home on the day the mob had gathered in Independence. Markley carried Matthew into a lean-to room in the back of Doc Noland's house and told Joseph to sit in the living room. It was a log house, but a big one with several rooms.

Joseph waited. He was tired and worried. He heard nothing from the back room. After a time Markley came out. "Doc says you can stay here with your brother tonight. Soon as he gets better we're gonna throw you both in jail." He left. Joseph doubted that he would see Markley again. Even though he could sound very tough, Joseph sensed that much of it had been show for the other men. Joseph felt certain that he would not come back to try to put them in jail.

Doc Noland eventually came out and told Joseph that Matthew's wound was not serious but that he had lost a good deal of blood and was very weak. He would be all right in a few days.

"Sir," Joseph said, "we have to get to our parents. We think they crossed into Clay County."

"Well, you can't travel for a few days. Maybe we can get word to your people somehow. Is it true that your brother hit Fred Brandt with an ax?"

"With the blunt end. But Mr. Brandt, or one of them, hit my father over the head with his rifle. My brother tried to fight the whole bunch with an ax, but they all had guns and one of them shot him."

"Well, that sounds about right. About what you could expect. You're the boy I talked to here in town last summer, aren't you?"

"Yes, sir."

"Well, I never thought it would come to this. I'm sorry. I suppose you will be better off somewhere else."

"If my father is alive."

"Yes." Noland stood and looked at Joseph for a moment, his brown eyes gazing intently on Joseph's face. "I'm sorry you have to go through this—especially at your age. I wish there were something I could say that would . . ." He stopped, seemingly looking for words. "My wife has dinner ready. Come in and eat. Your brother is sleeping, but I got a little soup into him. He just needs rest now."

Mrs. Noland was very nice. She seemed a strange wife for Doc Noland, not as articulate, apparently not as educated, but she was kind to Joseph. After dinner Joseph went in to see his brother. Matthew awoke for a few minutes and talked briefly with him. He wanted to know if anyone knew anything about their father. Joseph told him that he had not heard anything and Matthew nodded. He looked at Joseph questioningly, as though concerned about all Joseph's worries. "I think he will be all right. Try not to worry."

Joseph slept surprisingly well, and the next morning he was greatly encouraged to see Matthew eat a fairly good breakfast. Mrs. Noland helped Matthew, making sure he drank all his milk, which she had gone out early to get for him. Matthew sat up for a while after breakfast, and he and Joseph talked. They wanted Doc Noland to do something about getting word to the Saints as to where they were. He had gone out early, but they planned to talk to him about it when he got back. Matthew settled down to sleep again.

About ten o'clock that morning Doc Noland came home. He came to the room where Matthew was sleeping and Joseph was sitting. "Matthew," he said as he approached the bed. Matthew's eyes opened. "How do you feel?"

"Much better."

"That's good. I am afraid we have a problem." Noland looked serious and Joseph suddenly felt scared again. "Apparently the word has gotten around that you hit Brandt with an ax and that he is supposedly dying. I tried to explain what happened but they weren't about to listen. Some of these town ruffians are talking about—well, all kinds of things—and I don't think it will come to anything, but I am thinking it might be safest if I sneak you out of town now. If I could get you to your people they could take care of you. The ride in my wagon will be a little rough, but all in all that might be the safest course."

Joseph knew that the doctor was playing the danger down, just as his father always did. He felt his insides tighten up again. So they were still not out of danger.

Doc Noland and his wife bundled Matthew up. They gave him some breeches that belonged to Noland himself, and they were not all that much too big. And they gave him a heavy woolen shirt to wear under his old blanket coat. Both Matthew and Joseph had new boots, bought for the winter only recently. The Nolands helped Matthew put on his boots and stand up. With his arm around Doc Noland's shoulder for support, Matthew hobbled out to the back of the house, where Noland had left his wagon. The doctor got the boys to lie down in the back, and threw some quilts over them. Then the wagon bumped and creaked as the old team of mules began to plod ahead. They had barely started when Joseph heard a voice yelling in the distance somewhere, "He's helping them get away. He's got 'em in his wagon."

"Hold on," he heard Doc Noland say, cracking his whip. The mules picked up their pace and the wagon bounced along. Joseph had no idea where they were heading, but he dared not look up. The plan had been to head for the Independence landing where the Saints would probably be crossing the river on ferries, but now all Joseph knew was that Doc was making a run for it, and of course he wondered what would happen should they be stopped.

The wagon rattled ahead for some time, and finally Joseph peeked up. They were just barely out of town, but he could see no one following. Perhaps they were safe. But Doc was barking at the mules and they were trotting as hard as they could. Joseph ducked back under the quilt. "I can't see anyone behind us," he said to Matthew, but Matthew only groaned. Joseph clung to him to keep him as much as possible from bouncing, and for several minutes they continued on.

Then the wagon pulled up to a sudden stop, Doc Noland yelling "whoa" to his mules. In a moment he was by the boys, pulling the quilt away. "Get to the woods as fast as you can. I can hear horses coming fast." Joseph scurried down and helped Matthew get down as Doc jumped back onto the wagon. "Stay down," he yelled. "They'll follow me at first."

Matthew ran hard, to Joseph's surprise, and they were both quickly up an embankment and into the woods. They fell on their stomachs in the underbrush. In a short time they heard horses gallop by, several of them. Neither boy moved until the riders were well past.

Matthew finally rolled over onto his back. He was still breathing hard. "Are you all right?" Joseph asked.

"I'm tired," he said, and then he took another deep breath. "I was scared. I ran too fast."

"Just rest for a minute," Joseph said.

"What will we do, Joseph?"

"I think Doc wants us to stay here."

"But how can he come back for us? Won't they follow him?"

Joseph had no answer. They stayed in the brush, Joseph sitting up eventually, but not knowing what to do.

"Matthew," Joseph finally said, "I think we have to try to make it to the landing. It must be about five miles. If we stay off the road, in the woods, no one will see us. But we can watch the road and watch for Doc Noland."

"I can't, Joseph. I can't walk five miles."

"I'll help you, Matthew. You have to. If we sit here and Doc Noland can't come back for us, when night comes we could freeze."

"But Joseph . . ."

"Matthew, what else can we do? We have to try."

Joseph got up and helped Matthew to his feet. Joseph tried to help Matthew walk by getting under his arm, but Matthew wouldn't let him. "I can walk," he said. "But I'll have to take it slow, and I'll have to rest sometimes."

Joseph went ahead, trying to pick a path through the oak brush and sumac. Matthew followed, slowly, limping badly, and breathing in jerks, really little moans. In about three minutes he had to stop. "Rest," he said. He leaned against a tree, apparently not wanting to bend his leg. They had come only about fifty yards. They continued this way, a few minutes at a time, until they reached a downhill stretch where the oak brush was very thick. Joseph tried to hold back the limbs to clear the way for Matthew, but it was very difficult, and their progress was slow. And then Matthew's good leg simply gave out and he fell to the ground. "I can't, Joseph. I can't. We've hardly started. I could never—" He hesitated, catching his breath. "I could never make it five miles. And it might be more than that."

Joseph sat down also, not answering, but thinking. In a few minutes he heard a wagon. Maybe Doc was coming back. He hurried through the woods to a point where he could see the road. It was Doc, all right, but there were five horses with him. They had to be the men who had chased him, and now they were apparently escorting Doc back to town so he couldn't stop to pick up the boys again. The men were carefully studying the woods on both sides. Joseph fell on his stomach and let the riders go by; then he got up and went back to Matthew. When he told Matthew what he had seen, Matthew hung his head. Joseph was afraid his brother was going to cry.

"Listen, Matthew. We can walk on the road now. That will be easier. And you can lean on me."

Matthew looked up at Joseph. His face showed his discouragement. The firmness Joseph always expected from him was all gone. He looked defeated, his eyes sad and his jaw slack.

"Come on, Matthew. We've just got to try to make it."

Joseph got under Matthew's arm this time and they struggled to the road. They rested there and then started out. They could still only walk for three or four minutes at a time, but they could cover twice the distance. The problem, of course, was that this still wasn't much. It was fairly cold outside but Joseph was soon sweating. They didn't talk, just walked until Matthew's weight was too much for Joseph, or until Matthew gave up. Then Joseph would help Matthew sit down by the side of the road and they would build up their strength and catch their breaths.

They went on this way for an hour or more. Twice they hurried back into the woods when they heard horses coming, but they did not recognize the riders either time. The effort of the quick movement each time, however, took its toll, and afterwards Joseph noticed Matthew depending more on him, allowing more of his weight to rest on Joseph's shoulder.

The middle of the day came and went. Joseph knew that it would help greatly to have something to eat, but food was simply not available. Heavy clouds had been moving in from the northwest and gradually a light rain began to fall. The road became slick after a time, making the struggle up hills harder than ever. But they continued on. At times Matthew seemed only half-conscious. His breathing had become a series of grunts, and his eyes seemed not to focus on anything, not even when he sat to rest. "You are doing fine," Joseph kept saying. "We'll get there. We've come a long way." But they had not come far enough, and Joseph knew it. Joseph guessed that they were still not halfway there.

Finally Matthew simply couldn't last more than a

minute at a time, so Joseph suggested they take a longer rest. They sat for about twenty minutes, but the cold only stiffened them. Matthew made it a little further the first time, but after resting he could only last a minute or a minute and a half at a stretch again. Going uphill was terribly exhausting, but going downhill hurt Matthew's wound even more. And little of the land was flat.

"I can't, Joseph. I can't," Matthew said as they faced another hill, and he slumped in the road. Joseph tried to hold him but couldn't. Joseph's side was numb from holding up the weight, and his shoulder ached; he wanted to give up too. "Maybe someone will come," Matthew said after a few minutes of rest. "Maybe we can get a ride. Maybe some of the Independence members will come this way."

"I think they all came this way yesterday, Matthew. And the members from the Big Blue or west of it won't take this road."

"If someone else comes by, let's not hide. Let's ask for a ride. Some of them might be willing to help us."

"But it's getting afternoon, Matthew. Who would be coming out this way in the rain?"

"Maybe Doc Noland will come back."

"Maybe." But neither tried to get up. Joseph knew he had to do something soon, but he didn't know what. "Come on, Matthew, we can't wait for him. We have to keep going."

Joseph got up and helped Matthew up. He got under his shoulder and they started up the hill. Joseph felt stronger for the first twenty or thirty steps, but he began to ache all over again after that. Matthew was barely able to help himself. They only made it halfway up the hill, maybe not that far. Joseph let Matthew down and they both panted for about a minute. "All right. Let's go again. Let's make it to the top and then rest. Then we can make it down the other side easy. We'll just think about one hill at a time, all right, Matthew?"

Matthew didn't answer, but he struggled to his feet and

the two boys trudged ahead again. After going about thirty yards, Joseph slipped in the red dirt that was fast becoming mud, and down he went. After a few breaths he was ready again, tugging at Matthew. But they had barely begun before he slipped again, this time both of them falling face first. Matthew moaned. Joseph helped him roll over and held his head in his lap. Matthew looked pale. Joseph wondered whether he might be dying. A tear rolled down Matthew's cheek. Joseph knew he had to be strøng for Matthew. What would his father do? What would Joseph Smith do?

And then Joseph put his hands on Matthew's head, both of his hands, palms down. "Matthew Williams, in the name of Jesus Christ, I command you to arise," he said. He said it in a loud voice, a voice like the Prophet's, he hoped.

Matthew's eyes opened and he looked at Joseph, wonderingly. Joseph nodded to him confidently. Matthew, with Joseph's help, got up again and they made it to the top of the hill. But beyond it was another one, about like the one they had just reached the top of, only maybe a little higher. They rested, made it to the bottom in one walk, rested again, and started up the next hill. It took three strenuous attempts, but they made it to the top. Matthew seemed stronger than he had been for hours, and he was trying harder. His face tightened with each step and little moans came from his throat, but Joseph had to stop first each time.

They made it over three more hills and Joseph suspected that maybe they only had two miles to go. But he could also tell that some of Matthew's resolve was slipping away again. They said nothing to each other, concentrating on the work filling their minds totally. The light rain had become slightly heavier, and the wind blew it in their faces, but it was the mud that was the problem. It stuck to their boots now, making every step more effort than it would otherwise have been.

They had gone just a few steps up the next hill when Joseph felt Matthew give way gradually and begin to slip

134

away from him. He caught him, lowered him to the ground, and held his head again. "Matthew, I'll bless you again. Come on. We can't have too much farther to go. Matthew." There was no answer; Matthew was ashen. For a moment Joseph thought he was dead, but his chest was still rising and falling. "Matthew, can you hear me?" He had passed out, Joseph realized.

What could he do now? Maybe they were closer than he thought. Maybe he could go ahead and get help. No— he didn't dare leave Matthew. He was worried about wolves, but more than that he just could not stand to think of leaving his brother lying in the red mud, probably to die. "Oh, Father in heaven," he said aloud, "help me now. Help me. Make me strong." Then he got up, gripped Matthew under the arms, and started to pull, walking backwards. Matthew's bootheels dragged in the mud, making the going very difficult—even if Joseph had been fresh it would have been tough going. But he tugged a few steps at a time and then rested, only lowering Matthew's weight to the ground occasionally to rest his arms. He struggled backwards, his feet slipping in the mud. Twice he landed on his backside, but got back up and kept dragging. He inched his way up the hill, saying to himself only to think of the hill, nothing beyond. The downhill would be easier. Maybe the river was just over this hill, or the next one. Maybe they had come farther than it seemed.

It took a long time, at least half an hour, and it was getting close to dark, but Joseph made it to the top of the hill. Matthew was conscious at times and pleaded with Joseph to stop, but Joseph just kept pulling. "O Father, help me," he kept saying. "Don't let him die. Please don't let him die."

At the top of the hill he rested. He looked as far as he could see, but he could not tell where the river was. He could only see another hill, but a smaller one, and then one more after that. He decided that it might take him all night, but the effort would be better than giving up. He could not stop and give up. Going downhill, however, was very difficult. The load felt lighter, but the awkwardness was terrible. He slipped with almost every step, and once he dropped Matthew in the mud, splashing water over his head. "Oh, please don't, Joseph," Matthew said, distantly, and he lost consciousness again.

Joseph got a good rest before he tried the next hill. He began to feel cold, however, and he worried about Matthew and how cold he must be getting. So he got up and began to pull again. His strength was dwindling to nothing; he tugged and scratched and made only a few feet at a time. He realized he was crying, that he was in a state of panic, but he continued to mumble his prayers and to pull. He tried to dig his feet into the mud sideways for leverage, but time and again they slipped and he went down. Eventually he was hardly getting up, just pushing himself backwards on his backside and then tugging Matthew up to him. He made it up the little hill, but the sun was almost gone and now he knew that, though he might make it down, he would never be able to make it back up the next long hill, not even if it was the last one. And he knew that it probably was not.

Joseph held Matthew's head and cried and cried. Once he said, "Matthew, you must get up. I can't pull you any more." Matthew muttered something Joseph couldn't understand. Without even trying to get up, Joseph watched the sun disappearing. "Father," he finally said, "I can't do any more. I can't help it. Please help us make it the rest of the way somehow."

He decided once to give it another try, but found he just couldn't move any more. His bones ached, and his mind whirred when he tried to get up. So he sat and waited. About twenty minutes went by and it was very dark.

Then he heard a wagon. He let it come. If it was the enemy, then that was better than nothing. He waited until the wagon got close and then he yelled, "Stop. We're on the road and can't get up." He heard the wagon stop, and in a moment Doc Noland came out of the dark.

"Joseph. How did you get this far? I've been searching for you. I hoped you had gotten a ride to the river somehow."

"We walked. And then I pulled him for a while after he passed out."

"Oh, Joseph," Doc Noland said, his voice cracking, "I'm sorry. I'm so sorry. I tried to get back, but the men followed me. I had to wait all day."

"We almost made it, Doctor Noland," Joseph said. "But I just couldn't go any further."

"How bad is Matthew?"

"He's alive. But he keeps passing out."

Doc Noland picked Matthew up and put him in the wagon. Joseph got up and made it to the wagon, but he was too weak to climb up. Noland helped Joseph into the back of the wagon and the boy sat by Matthew, cradling his head in his lap.

It turned out to be less than a mile to the landing where many of the Saints were camped along the Missouri waiting for their turn to cross on the ferries. They had set up crude shelters and built fires, which they tried to keep going in spite of the rain. Doc Noland carried Matthew to one of the shelters and helped to get some warm clothes on him, feed him, and redress the wound. Joseph was wrapped in a warm blanket and given a place by the fire. He too had some supper and then curled up to sleep near Matthew. He slept fitfully, however, seeing in his dreams the red mud, the blackness descending over the hills, Matthew's white face. But once, when he awoke, he realized again that it was over, that they had made it. He felt satisfied with his effort, overwhelmed with thankfulness that, when he had done all he could, the end had not come. He saw in his mind the picture of Doc Noland coming out of the darkness, heard him say, "Oh, Joseph, I'm sorry," heard his voice break with emotion, and then Joseph cried.

Chapter 17

The next morning Joseph felt different, changed. It was as though all his past life had died and something new now had to begin. He already felt something new within himself, in fact. He felt stronger, older, less frightened. He had learned some things, although he was not certain that he could put any of them into words, nor did he try.

All morning the Saints waited as the rain poured down. Gradually more and more were moving across the river as increasing numbers of ferries were called into action. No one seemed to know where the Colesville people were, but it was assumed that they had crossed further to the west near the mouth of the Big Blue River.

Matthew ate a little bit and then slept again. He was exceedingly weak, but his life was no longer flickering. Finally a man came and carried him to the ferry, and Joseph followed. The Missouri was boiling, and the swift current carried the ferry a long way to the east. Then it had to be poled along the shore back to where the Saints had made camp. It took almost two hours to make the crossing. Joseph saw to it that Matthew was sheltered as soon as they reached the shore, and then he began searching for his parents.

The Saints were camped in temporary shelters much as they had been on the other side of the river, except that the brethren had been felling cottonwood trees. Rugs and blankets, bits of canvas, tree boughs, whatever the Saints could find, were strewn across these shanties, but they leaked terribly and people huddled together for warmth as they watched the rain pour down. No one had seen Joseph's parents, but someone said that the Colesville members were camped further up the river. Joseph continued on along the river to the west until he eventually saw another encampment. As he approached he saw Newel Knight helping some other brethren tie down a covering over a little shelter. They were all soaked, their broad-brimmed hats drooping and their coats sopping wet. Joseph yelled to Brother Knight and he turned around.

"Joseph! Thank heaven," he said as Joseph ran to him. Brother Knight grabbed him in his arms. "We thought we had lost you. They forced us to leave without you. Where's Matthew?"

"He got shot, but he's alive. He's up the shore. Where's father? Is he alive?"

"Yes, but he's not well, Joseph. He was hurt seriously, and he had to make it here on foot. We helped him, but it was a terrible ordeal. But he will live. Don't worry about that."

Brother Knight embraced Joseph again as the rain pelted down on them, and then he took Joseph to the little shanty where his parents were. His mother was on her knees, bending over Brother Williams. She looked up and saw Joseph. "Oh, Joseph," she said. "Joseph." Her eyes filled with tears as she pulled him to her and hugged his wet coat to her face. "Is Matthew all right? Where is he?"

"He's all right, Mother, but he got shot in the leg. But we made it. He's down the river in the other camp."

Joseph felt a hand touch his arm and he looked down at his father. Brother Williams looked pale and weak, much like Matthew. "You did well, son," his father said, his voice a whisper.

"What did they do to you, Father?"

"Oh, Joseph," his mother said, "they came back and beat him—kicked him, broke his ribs, and hurt him inside."

"I'll be fine," Brother Williams said.

And then Mother held Joseph again. Joseph felt that the baby had still not come, that his mother had suffered awfully, but he also recognized a change. She was the mother he had missed for months.

Brother Knight went with Joseph, and they brought Matthew back and put him in the shelter alongside his father. That night, as the rain dripped around her and sisters knelt by her side, Sister Williams gave birth to her third son, a big boy, strong and healthy.

Everyone in the family was down now, except for Joseph and Ruth. The sisters helped, and, as the sun came out and began to dry the wet shelters, the brethren worked hard building better cabins along the shores of the river and among the cottonwoods. Joseph brought food to his family, helped them eat, and watched their strength begin to return. The three invalids were side by side in the little shelter. One of the sisters had taken Ruth and another cared for the baby, bringing him to Sister Williams to be fed.

Joseph watched his parents and Matthew get stronger each day. His mother had suffered much more than just the delivery of a baby. She was fatigued from the worry and the terror and the cold. But she recovered quickly, and Joseph saw in her the strength that she had once told him she could possess. Joseph knew that she had resolved to meet the challenges ahead, to start over again. He was not sure why, except that she seemed very thankful to at least have her family all alive.

Matthew was up walking in three days, surprising everyone. At first it was hard for him to talk to Joseph. He was embarrassed; he found it difficult to tell his brother all he felt. He thanked him, of course, but Joseph could tell that Matthew felt something stronger than he was able to express. Finally he asked Joseph one day, "When I begged you to quit, why didn't you?"

"I don't know, Matthew. I kept thinking about what it would be like if you were gone from us. That made me not want to give up."

Matthew looked at the ground, still avoiding Joseph's eyes, and said, "Now you can see why Joseph Smith told you that you would be a great man."

"I don't know, Matthew. I finally did quit when I just

140

couldn't—well, you know what happened."

"But you showed what you could do, Joseph. Not many would have stayed with it the way you did. I wanted to quit long before you did. You are strong, Joseph."

But Joseph still didn't want to talk about that. He just wanted to work as hard as he could to get a new house built somewhere if it turned out they couldn't return to their old one, and he wanted to carry as much of the load as he could until his father was back to full strength. His father was recovering very slowly. He got up sometimes, but not for long. He never expressed any discouragement, but Joseph could see that his resolve had been at least momentarily weakened, and the rest of the family would have to furnish the strength for a time.

About a week went by before the whole family was finally moved into a crude, windowless cabin along with several other families. Many of the Saints had fallen ill and warmth was badly needed. The cabin was temporary but reasonably warm, and a great improvement over the cold shelters they had been getting by with. The plan was to manage for the winter somehow and then worry about the future. Everyone hoped to get help soon and return to Jackson County, but few really believed it would happen in the near future.

Brother Higbee managed to sneak back into Jackson County and get a rifle he had hidden, and he was able to shoot several deer, helping greatly to feed the Saints. Gradually more of the members were filtering into Clay County. Some, it turned out, had gone south into Van Buren County, and for many years people in the area told of tracking this little group by following the trail of blood. The children's shoeless feet had been cut by the bunch grass on the burnt prairie. Lyman Wight was still missing and his wife had given birth to a son since the time he had been chased from their home. Philo Dibble, who had been all but given up, with a bullet in his abdomen, had been blessed by Newel Knight, had expelled the bullet along with the infection, and had gotten up and walked from the

141

county with the others. But Brother Barber was dead, and many others who had been beaten were still not well.

The second night after moving into the cabin the Williamses were awakened by a knocking on the cabin door. Fear was naturally Joseph's first response, but then he heard Brother Knight's voice: "Get up, everyone. There is something you all must see."

At first Brother Williams did not get up with the others, but Brother Knight came in and asked him to, helped him up, and took him outside. It was cold, and everyone wrapped themselves with blankets and stood together in front of the cabin. In the sky streaks of light were flashing about: long green streaks of light, dozens at a time, almost like fireworks.

"Falling stars," Joseph said, but it was inadequate. Never had he seen such a thing. At times it was almost as light as day outside. The display continued for a long time, sometimes seeming almost to stop, then bursting forth with a hundred flashes at once. The Saints watched in awe, talking quietly, sighing in one breath when the flashes were most intense.

Father continued to lean on Brother Knight, with Matthew close by. Mother held Joseph close to her. Ruth and the baby were asleep.

"Brother Williams," Joseph heard Brother Knight say, "I can't help thinking this is a sign to us. I think it is God's way of saying that he is still with us, that we should not forget the greatness of his power. We have gone through a terrible trial, a test of our faith and strength, but he will not abandon us."

It crossed Joseph's mind that what had happened in Jackson County certainly seemed like abandonment. But he did not bring it up. He did not know whether this was a sign from God, but he felt a sense that something of great power was occurring before his eyes, and, more importantly, he had a new feeling that he had learned to tap some of that power.

Brother Knight decided to see if everyone had gotten

142

up to see the rain of stars. He let Joseph take his father's weight. They stood for some time hardly noticing the cold and not speaking at all. Joseph enjoyed the sense that he was now strong enough to give his father some support.

As had happened many times since he had crossed the river out of Zion, Joseph found himself thinking about his friend Ollie. He wondered where he was, whether he was watching the falling stars. He wished that he could talk to Ollie, thank him. He didn't say it to himself, because he didn't have the idea very clearly formulated, but he hoped somehow that Ollie felt some of the same strength—and the same smallness—under the same stars.